A
SINGULAR
CONSPIRACY

A Singular Conspiracy

* * *   * * *

By BARRY PEROWNE

The Bobbs-Merrill Company, INC.
INDIANAPOLIS / NEW YORK

"Assassinate General Aupick!"
> —Charles Baudelaire, inciting a
> revolutionary Paris street mob
> against his own stepfather.

*"For the first four months of 1844 the whereabouts
and doings of Edgar Allan Poe cannot be satisfactorily traced."*
> —Various biographers

A

SINGULAR

CONSPIRACY

One

Paris, eve of the New Year 1844, and a thin rain falling.

Hoofs clopped, the lamps of passing carriages glimmered wanly, wheels splashed through puddles as a twenty-four-year-old boulevardier in silk hat, purple-lined cloak and a dandy's pink silk gloves paid off a fiacre in front of the steps of the Théâtre du Panthéon.

Gold-knobbed stick in one hand, a bouquet of rosebuds in the other, he walked into the alley alongside the theatre and picked his way fastidiously over the greasy cobbles to where a lanthorn containing a lugubrious blue gas jet sputtered over the stage door.

He went in, closed the door behind him, and said, *"Bonsoir, Jacques."*

The doorkeeper, on his high stool embowered among old theatre bills behind his loge counter, was drinking beer from a jug and leafing through a pile of dog-eared newsprint. He wiped malted froth from a discouraged moustache with the back of his hand.

"*Bonsoir,* Monsieur Baudelaire. You're early tonight. Mademoiselle Duval's still on."

"So I hear."

Muted from the auditorium sounded the ballet music of *Sheba and the Beast,* and, through a tangle of dangling ropes and between painted flats that leaned shadowy against the walls, Charles Baudelaire caught a glimpse of his mistress on the lighted stage.

Sinuous in the dance that invited, tantalized and gracefully eluded the clutches of a tumescent gorilla, her perfect body, barefoot and ankleted, shimmered like burnished ebony through the swirl of her diaphanous garment; the dagger in her hand and the crescent of the regal diadem that secured her raven hair caught the light with a wicked glitter.

Baudelaire's fine dark eyes followed her until the choreography of the ballet, long familiar to him, whirled her from his view. He glanced at the ribboned bouquet he carried. The rosebuds, dewed lightly by the rain, were the hue of rich cream, and he could see them, in anticipation, as presently Jeanne would hold them to the dusk of her breasts and, inhaling the scent of the roses, look at him over them with a hint of mockery in the slant of her amber eyes.

He smiled sardonically. Jealousy was always mocked by the desired one who evoked it; and though, with his pale, cleanly chiseled features and his trim beard, silkily black, Baudelaire was strikingly handsome, yet where Jeanne Duval was concerned he was jealous of every potent male—above all, currently, that lurching and hirsute beast gibbering erotically through brutish fangs.

"You read English, Monsieur Baudelaire?"

"English?" Baudelaire turned to the doorkeeper. "I learned something of that plummy tongue at the maternal knee, Jacques. My mother squandered the bloom of her youth philandering in the foggy drawing rooms of London society. She picked up English, but turned down Englishmen. God is sometimes merciful."

Or *was* He? It might have been better for himself, Baudelaire thought wryly, if with her second marriage his mother, Caroline, had inflicted on him, for a stepfather, some roaring English squire belching port wine and reeking of the stables, rather than that hawk-nosed ramrod of the military virtues, General Aupick of the French Ministry of War.

"Someone left these papers lying around in a dressing room," said Jacques.

Baudelaire laid his bouquet and ebony-sheathed swordstick on the counter and with pink-gloved hands leafed distastefully through the papers.

"These are American, Jacques—transatlantic periodicals about six months out of date."

"Then it was that soprano we had here last week, Monsieur Baudelaire. *She* must have left them. She was from America."

"An American soprano? She was well advised to trill in greener pastures, Jacques. Her high notes, be they never so pure, would be wasted on her compatriots' ears, which are notoriously deaf to all melody except that of the tills in their counting-houses. See here, for instance, the name of this ineffable journal—*The Dollar Newspaper*. How typical! How artlessly mercantile!"

"Is American the same as English, Monsieur Baudelaire?"

"It is to English, Jacques, as the speech of Normandy is to French."

"Ah, *les Normands*," said Jacques, enlightened.

"Rudimentary," Baudelaire agreed. "Now, what have we here? An example, it seems, of transatlantic literature." With the condescension of avowedly aesthetic youth, he read aloud from the small print that covered with daunting density the front page of *The Dollar Newspaper,* " 'A good glass in the bishop's hostel in the devil's seat—' "

"That's American?" said Jacques. "You read it like a native, monsieur."

"It takes practice," Baudelaire said, and continued reading, " 'Forty-one degrees and fourteen minutes—northeast and by north. Main branch seventh limb east side—' "

"Does it mean anything?" Jacques asked.

"One wonders," said Baudelaire. " 'Shoot from the left eye of the death's head—' Dear me, from the desert of *beaux arts* a cryptic voice gives tongue! To find out what about—if anything comprehensible—one looks to the beginning. Ah-hah! 'The Gold Bug.' By Edgar A. Poe.' "

"Bug? *Qu'est-ce que c'est* 'bug,' monsieur?"

"I'll see if the insidious Mr. Poe enlightens us, Jacques."

Baudelaire pushed his silk hat further back on his head and, leaning with graceful elegance against the counter, began indulgently to read, though not now aloud, the tale in *The Dollar Newspaper.*

It was quite a long tale.

Jacques finished his beer, filled a short clay pipe with black tobacco and, holding the pipe upside down between his two upper teeth and three lower, sucked it alight over the wire-caged gas jet which more or less illumined his loge. He resumed his seat on the weary cushion of his stool.

From the auditorium came, after a while, the crescendo of the finale, merging into the clapping of approving palms.

"Curtain calls, Monsieur Baudelaire," said Jacques.

Baudelaire nodded absently, reading on, a lock of black hair falling aslant across his pale brow.

"Mademoiselle's flowers," Jacques reminded him, for usually Monsieur Baudelaire was waiting in the wings, flowers in hand, when mademoiselle came off.

But Baudelaire went on reading, and Mademoiselle Jeanne,

coming offstage attended by the gorilla, put her dagger on the props table and looked around expectantly.

"Monsieur," Jacques whispered.

Jeanne saw Baudelaire then, deep in his reading as he leaned with an elbow on the loge counter, the gold chain of his cloak unfastened, his suit-coat sky blue, his waistcoat primrose, a pearl in his cravat, a pink-gloved finger propping his fine forehead, and his legs, in perfectly cut pearl-gray trousers, becomingly crossed at the ankles.

Jeanne looked hard for a moment at her inattentive paramour, then said something to the gorilla, who turned prominent canines, and eye sockets deep-sunken under bone ridges, in Baudelaire's direction.

Jeanne shrugged and passed from Jacques's view. She was dogged by the hairy brute, who, though no longer bent at the knees and pounding his great chest in sexual bafflement, gave no impression of honorable intentions toward her.

Jacques said softly, "He's gone to her dressing room with her, Monsieur Baudelaire. He'll get her to help him off with his head, no doubt."

Baudelaire went on reading.

"*And* his hide," Jacques added meaningly. "Oh, *la, la!*"

But Baudelaire went on reading.

Members of the orchestra started coming up the wooden steps from their pit, carrying their instruments in their cases, and in a hurry to wet their whistles.

"*A demain,* Jacques," they said as they passed the doorkeeper. "*Bonsoir,* Monsieur Baudelaire."

"*Au revoir,*" said Jacques as the thirsty melodists went out into the drizzle of the alley. "*Prenez garde,* messieurs."

Bubbling his pipe, Jacques looked curiously at Baudelaire, for usually it was he who took care—close care—of his mistress. He was jealous about her—everyone knew it—and he had plenty of cause, as everyone also knew, and none better than the gorilla.

But there, what could you expect of a black lady from some godforsaken island in the Indian Ocean or some such place where they hadn't sense enough to come in out of the sun?

Jacques shrugged a shoulder and had another jug of beer. Mademoiselle was monsieur's problem.

Baudelaire drew a long, slow breath.

"Well, well," he said. "Well, well, well!"

He stood looking down thoughtfully at *The Dollar Newspaper,* then glanced about him. It had become very quiet. In the stillness, beer glugged down Jacques's throat from the bottle. Jacques wiped his moustache.

"Curtain's down, monsieur. Mademoiselle's dressing."

Baudelaire tossed a coin onto the counter. "Jacques, you won't want these papers." He picked up his stick and the pile of newsprint, started to turn away.

"And these, monsieur?"

Baudelaire turned back. Jacques held out the bouquet to him.

"And the 'bug'?" said Jacques. "You were going to tell me—"

But Baudelaire took the bouquet and walked away through the shadows to Jeanne Duval's dressing room.

He knocked on the door and went in.

A gas jet, wire-caged, quivered a bluish flame, fan-shaped, above the mirror, before which Jeanne, in her flimsy garment, was sitting on a cushioned stool. Costumes hung around on rails, and on the cluttered shelf under the mirror stood the gorilla's head. The gorilla himself, in his hairy hide laced up the back, was leaning against the wall of indifferently whitewashed bricks, talking to Jeanne.

Devoid of his brute's head, the gorilla was clean shaven and handsome from the neck up. He was wiping burnt-cork circles from around his eyes with a much-daubed towel.

"*Bonsoir,* Baudelaire," he said.

Baudelaire ignored him. He dropped a kiss on the top of

Jeanne's sleek head, which smelled of sandalwood, and the bouquet into her lap. She went on with her toilette, not looking at him, her eyes dreaming at her reflection, full-lipped and Arab-fine in its features, flickering there in the smeared mirror.

"*Alors,*" said the gorilla, tossing his towel onto the ledge. "*Au revoir, tous les deux.*"

He reached for the gorilla head of papier-mâché, but Baudelaire poked the ferrule of his stick between the protruding fangs and, holding the head out to its owner, met his eyes fleetingly—amused eyes, knowing eyes, taunting eyes.

"*Merci,*" said the gorilla with a bow, "*mon cher* Baudelaire!"

He went out, laced up his hairy back, his head under his arm.

Baudelaire put the pile of newsprint on the shelf under the mirror and used his stick to gingerly pick up the gorilla's towel and, with a grimace, drop it into a frayed wicker wastebasket.

"You're in a mood, I see," said Jeanne, "—because Santoin was in here, I suppose."

"Your taste, though quite execrable, Jeanne," said Baudelaire, "has nothing to do with my mood, which happens to be a good mood—a most excellent mood."

"Which means you're thinking of something nasty," said Jeanne, smoothing unguent on her cheeks. "What a mind you have, Charles!"

"A mind open, as any poet's should be, to all experience," said Baudelaire. "And I've just *had* an experience, Jeanne—a rare and enriching one!"

"What new perversion have you discovered now?"

"I've discovered a microbe—and its master," said Baudelaire. "A great but unknown master, Jeanne! And I fancy I'm the first Frenchman to have discovered him, this master of the microbe—and the macabre!"

"Charles, what are you talking about?"

"A bug," said Baudelaire. "And it's bitten me."

"Evidently," said Jeanne.

"A unique bug—a most sinister bug," said Baudelaire. "A transatlantic bug."

In high spirits he swept off his silk hat, clapped it onto Jeanne's head. And they made a handsome couple, black and white in the mirror there, the dancer and the dandy, as he leaned over her with his pink-gloved hands on her shoulders and his dark eyes vivacious on her reflected image.

"A *gold* bug," said Baudelaire, exultant.

Two

Far away in New York, and far, far from exultant on this eve of the New Year 1844, the master of the microbe sat alone at a small table in the saloon of a waterfront tavern.

His black suit threadbare, thinning curls clustered about his prominent brow, his eyes cavernous and his pallor extreme, he was sketching idly with a sliver of charred stick on the back of an old handbill.

On a spare chair at the table were his caped gray greatcoat and tall black beaver hat, and nearby stood a pot-bellied stove from the interstices of which crawled worms of smoke whenever the wind gusted icily in the chimney pipe.

The sketch taking rough shape under his hand was a nostalgic reminiscence of one small triumph, one small oasis in a desert of defeats. It was an insect, a death's head scarab—a bug. But his thoughts were not on it. His sliver of charcoal moved of its own volition, for into his mind, preoccupied with his troubles, which were legion, there had encroached, God knew why, a scene from God alone knew whence, not Poe.

Who were these revelers in medieval motley and a wild dance? All Poe knew was that what inspired their frenzied gyrations and strident merriment was a seeking for forgetfulness of the presence of plague in their contaminated city.

He frowned, his sliver of charcoal stilled. What city *was* this? And where? His eyes blank to all but the theatre in his head, Poe watched the wild dancers freeze one by one to immobility as they became aware of a figure that stalked slowly among them—a stranger, garbed in crimson, a dagger belted at his hip, his face pale and still and coldly beautiful.

The charcoal moved, neatly printing: "Masque of the Red Death."

Poe blinked. Contemplating the words he had written on the handbill, he wondered if there was a usable title there, a possible idea which, resourcefully developed, maybe could be bartered for a few dollars of eating money—and a drink or two.

He swallowed, reminded again of the chronic dryness of his throat, and glanced at the glass at his elbow. It was empty. It had been empty far too long. But just then a latch rattled, and the door flew open to admit the wind of a wild night. The pendant lamps rocked on their chains and a cloud of smoke from the stove enveloped Poe and set him coughing.

"Shut that goddam door!" a voice roared.

Coughing painfully into the handkerchief clapped to his thin black moustache, Poe saw a man in the doorway. Behind him, a cab stood on the potholed street under the reaching bowsprits of ships tied up along the waterfront with the wind plucking a banshee shrill from their rigging.

Forcing the door shut against the gale, the newcomer turned

with an apology to the group of men from whose table, littered with playing cards and cash, the peremptory shout had come.

"Your pardon, gentlemen."

Neither the men around the table nor the gaudy wench standing with an arm resting proprietorially on the shoulder of the dealer, shuffling the cards, paid the newcomer any heed.

"You're shy, Sam," said the dealer.

"Huh?"

"Come on, come on! If you're comin' in, ante up!"

"Slick Sam with a dollar, ain't he, Nate?" said the wench.

"You go to hell, Mag," Sam suggested to her, and sullenly produced his stake.

Nate started to deal the deck as the newcomer walked across to the bar. Tall, young, good-looking, his traveling cap and ulster proclaiming him a man of substance, he put a small grip on the bar, remarking mildly, "They've got quite a pot on the table there."

"New Year's Eve," said the landlord, polishing glasses; "bonus night for dock hands."

"Some night! How about a hot buttered rum and a warm bed?"

"Specialties of The Shamrock House, mister. That all your baggage?"

"That's it. I'm sailing for Europe tomorrow, and my trunk's gone aboard."

"Mag!" the landlord called, and the girl deserted the gamblers and came to the bar. "Take the gent's grip up to Number Eight."

Mag looked at the label tied to the grip. "Henry Lane Duprez, New Orleans," she said, reading the label. "Passenger to Vigo. Where's Vigo, mister?"

"It makes no odds where Vigo is," said the landlord severely. "Take that grip up to Number Eight—an' pass a warmin' pan through the bed."

Mag gave Duprez a speculative look, but she took the grip

and moved away to a door between sleazy velvet curtains looped back by cords.

The landlord, pushing a steaming glass across the bar to Duprez, improved his geography by inquiring, "Where's Vigo, mister?"

Poe, hearing this from his table over by the stove, knew very well where Vigo was. He knew his Spain. His copy of *Don Quijote de la Mancha*, well-thumbed, was back there in Philadelphia—unless Mrs. Clemm, his aunt and mother-in-law, had pawned it to help out during the recent bad time that had forced him to leave for New York in search of journalistic employment.

At the thought of Maria Clemm and of Virginia, his cousin —his seventeen-year-old wife—Poe's brows contracted as to a stab of pain. They were not the least of his troubles, those two, well loved by him—and left by him, left in poverty and watching every mail, back there in Philadelphia, for word from him.

Oh, God, the burdens of conscience!

To exorcise them, he forced his mind back to *Don Quijote* and that book's creator, Cervantes de Saavedra, a man after Poe's own heart—a man of the pen *and* of the sword. He imagined himself walking with Cervantes, veteran of Lepanto, where he had lost an arm fighting under Don Juan of Austria. They walked together, Edgar Poe, sometime of West Point, and Cervantes of Lepanto, through Spanish caves, *bodegas*, lit by the naked flare of torches in iron sconces on rock walls ranked round with pyramids of sherry casks on wooden trestles.

"Two men," said Cervantes gruffly, "with a soldier's honest thirst! Now, here—here's a fine wine of Jerez, fifty years in the *solera*. A prime *amontillado!* How say you, Edgar—shall we sample this one?"

"Willingly, my dear Miguel," Poe said, noting that the old hero, despite his loss of an arm, handled a pipette well enough to milk a cask deftly.

"Pardon me, sir," said a strange voice.

Poe came out of his muse with a start, looking up, gulping with a dry throat as he saw before him a steaming glass held in a steady hand. Poe's gaze followed the steam upward and met the smile of Henry Lane Duprez, standing close by, warming his tail before the pot-bellied stove.

"Oh! I'm sorry," Duprez said, seeming disconcerted by Poe's stare. "I fear I've broken in on your reverie."

"My reverie?" said Poe. He shrugged. "A short walk, sir, in Dementia."

"Unmapped territory," said Duprez, "fraught with pitfalls." He emptied his glass. "Pray be my guest, sir, and let's celebrate your return in this hot buttered rum. It's excellent, I assure you."

"No further recommendation," said Poe, with a wintry smile, "is necessary."

"Landlord," Duprez called, "two rums!"

"Take a seat," said Poe cordially, and made to move his greatcoat and hat from the spare chair.

But Duprez forestalled him. "Let me!" Lifting Poe's things onto a neighboring table, he remarked, "Ah, a West Point greatcoat, I see."

Uneasiness seized Poe. He had been expelled from West Point, through his own deliberate action in a weak moment, and had often regretted it.

He gave Duprez a searching look. "You're at the Academy?"

"No, sir, I have not that honor, but I know a West Point greatcoat when I see one."

"A relic of my youth," said Poe, relieved that Duprez was not a West Point alumnus. "I'm on the wrong side of thirty now, and traveling—for my health."

"Where away, sir?"

"No gentleman," said Poe, "needs to know where he is going—only where he is from."

He began to tear up his sketch.

"I was about to venture a question," said Duprez. "That—uh—black beetle—one of our American species, may I ask?"

"Not so. It was hatched, this bug," Poe explained, "in the womb of Invention, the daughter of Necessity, for the purpose of activating a brief chronicle. Nothing is so dead as a last year's tale. Only the decades can restore it to critical respectability."

He tossed the fragments into the cinder tray under the stove.

"The moral," he said, "is plain: 'Tell it not in Gath nor publish it on the streets of Askelon—' "

" 'Lest the daughters of the Philistine rejoice—' " said Duprez.

" 'And the sons of the uncircumcised be made glad,' " Poe said. "Precisely, sir!"

"Two rums," said the landlord, putting the steaming glasses on the table.

"Your health," said Duprez, clinking his glass against Poe's.

"And yours," said Poe.

They drank.

"Excellent," Poe said, with a grateful sigh. "In the main, of course, frugality is the armor of the artist. He must needs show to the world an unmoved face, stonily inscrutable—even though, such is his nature, the ganglions of his being vibrate sensitively to every wind that blows."

"And listen to that one," said Duprez with a shudder, as the gale wuthered audibly in the chimney pipe. "By God, I dread the thought of it tomorrow, off Sandy Hook!"

"Bound for Europe, I heard you say."

"By a limejuicer," said Duprez—"the British ship *Ludgate Hill*, now lading. A journey for love's sake, I may say."

"For love's sake," Poe said, "a man might dare anything—even an act of oblivion."

He thought fleetingly of his father, the father he had been too young to know—his father: the actor, the mountebank, the mummer, who, committing just such an act of oblivion, had walked out of a theatre one night with his greasepaint on and, leaving Poe's mother, an actress, to die neglected, had never been heard from again.

"Oblivion?" Duprez said.

Poe thought of the man, wealthy Mr. Allan, merchant, of Richmond, Virginia, who had adopted him—adopted him and then, disillusioned, severed all contact. Cruel life! Not one cent would Mr. Allan part with now if he knew it might fall into Poe's hands. But with Poe gone, Mr. Allan—pious Mr. Allan—would never permit Virginia, if Mrs. Clemm appealed to him, to languish frail and hungering in Philadelphia. His righteousness, his stern sense of responsibility for an erring foster son's child-wife, would not permit it.

Poe said, with a bitter smile, "There are times, young sir, when a man's loved ones could be better off for . . . his act of oblivion." He patted his pockets. "I thought I had some cigars on me, but—"

"Try one of mine," Duprez said, "a weed from my father's plantation."

"Rolled," Poe asked, accepting the cigar, "on the naked thighs of an octoroon?"

"You touch upon a sore point, sir," Duprez said.

He leaned from his chair to ignite a stick at the bars of the stove.

"Mr. Duprez," Mag called, returning through the doorway with the draped curtains, "your bed's ready when you are."

With a flirt of her shawl tassels, she went back to the gamblers' table and, a possessive hand on Nate's broad shoulder, stood there watching again.

Poe, with neither bed nor warming pan in prospect and just one dollar and a few cents in his pocket, took comfort from the cigar he lighted carefully at the flame of the stick Duprez held for him.

"My Lady Nicotine," said Poe, puffing, "mistress of en-during charms!" He inhaled deeply, but with care because of his cough, closing his eyes the better to savor the fragrant smoke. "Europe," he murmured. "Now, I—if *I* were there—I'd seek out the headquarters of the Lafayette Circle—"

"The late great Marquis?" Duprez said, lighting his own cigar.

"Dead these ten years," said Poe, "but his admirers have formed, under the nose of King Louis-Philippe, an association of freedom-lovers. They have influence in high places." His eyes opened, kindling. "I'd seek it to obtain me some small command in the army of Poland, struggling in the clutch of the Russian bear. Fit work there for an American sword!"

"But your health, sir?"

"Ennui, for the most part," said Poe, "and action is the physic for it!"

"I admire your ardor," said Duprez. "For my part, what takes me to Europe is—romance. I was engaged briefly—all too briefly. A Miss Kate Casteign, sir, daughter of a British diplomat deceased while *en poste* in Washington, D.C. Kate and her mother moved subsequently to Williamsburg—"

"A Tory stronghold!"

"And Lady Casteign's a true-blue Tory—preserved in tea and lavender water!" Duprez puffed ruefully at his cigar. "I mentioned just now—h'm—a sore point."

"Naked thighs, if I recall?"

"A wench on the old plantation," Duprez confessed. "I was, in a sense, entangled. A wild oat, no more."

"A gentleman's birthright," Poe said.

"Unfortunately, the matter came to light in awkward cir-cumstances. I won't conceal from you, sir," said Duprez, "that a scene occurred. Lady Casteign, being British, doesn't really un-derstand the American way of life. My engagement to Kate was broken off. My ring was returned, and Lady Casteign promptly spirited Kate away to Europe. I've written her many letters there—contrite, explanatory—in care of various British Consulates."

"No reply?"

"Not a word!" said Duprez. "But I had news recently from a mutual friend that Kate and her mother are wintering in Spain."

"So you go to seek them out?"

"I *must!* It's my only hope. I love her!" Duprez took a document from his pocket, slapped the paper down on the table. "And there it is—my last chance, my gamble—the document for my passage to Vigo, and I'm banking on it!"

"I sympathize with your emotion," Poe said. "But, as a man ten years your senior, all passion spent, I myself view life in the cold light of logic. Cause and effect. Every situation—"

"Cheat!"

The wild shout and the clatter of a chair violently overturned interrupted Poe.

"Signals, by God!" It was Sam the sullen, on his feet at the gamblers' table and raging now at Mag. "You tipped my hand to Nate!"

"No, Sam! How could I? You're crazy!"

"You bin doin' it right along," Sam yelled, "tappin' out signals on his shoulder, you draggle-drawered harlot!"

"That's enough, Sam," Nate said stonily. "Sit down or get out!"

"You bet I'll get out—an' I'm takin' that pot with me!"

"Think again, Sam!"

"Easy, now!" bawled the landlord, alarmed. "Easy on, fellers!"

"I want my money," Sam shouted, "an' I'm takin it!"

Nate's hand flashed from his pocket. "Stand back, Sam! Let that pot alone!"

"No guns!" yelled the landlord. "No guns!"

Sam made a dive at Nate's throat across the table, which collapsed in splintering ruin as the small pistol in Nate's hand went off with a sharp report.

Mag screamed, pointing at Duprez as he put both hands to his chest, looked with stupefaction at the blood on them, then bowed slowly forward over the table before the cavernous eyes of Poe.

Three

Dimly, Poe was conscious of a stampede of booted feet across the saloon floor, the rattle of a latch, the bang of the street door flung open by the icy wind sweeping in, salty and boisterous like a drink-maddened sailor, setting the lamps asway and the shadows wildly rocking. Smoke belched from the stove.

"Wait!" the landlord bellowed. "Come back here!" But he might as well have saved his breath. "Gone, the bastards!"

He flung up the flap of his bar, ran to the street door, forced it shut against the wind, and bolted it. He turned, flushed and furious.

"It wasn't me!" Mag wailed. "I never done nothing!"

"Quit screechin'," said the landlord, and came to Poe's table. "Where'd it hit him, mister?"

Poe wheezed, coughing, "In the midst of life—"

"Bastards! Bastards!" said the landlord. "New Year's Eve! A foul night like this, I thought we'd have it quiet for once. Always some goddam thing! Mag, go out the back way—run for Doc Halloran."

"He's here. He come in earlier, with that woman."

"Go pull him off her. *Run*, damn you!"

Mag ran.

"So this—" Poe said sepulchrally, his eyes on Duprez sitting jackknifed forward over the table, his arms limply dangling, his cigar fallen to the floor "—so this is New York."

The landlord gave him a sharp look. "Stranger in town?"

"Got in today," Poe said, "from Philadelphia by the Perth Amboy railroad route."

"Too bad you run into this! How about a drink?"

"It would settle the nerves," Poe admitted, "now that the clouds of battle have cleared."

The landlord went to the bar. Poe, coughing into his handkerchief, picked up Duprez's half-smoked cigar.

"A nail in whose coffin?" he wondered, looking at the motionless young tobacco planter—and, pressing out the cigar's glow, pocketed the stub.

The landlord came back with a bottle, filled the glasses. They drank.

"Taken and wanted," said the landlord, refilling the glasses. "Better not try givin' this gent none, I guess."

"Better leave him to the doctor," Poe agreed, "—or the undertaker."

Into his mind drifted a memory of an English etching he once had seen, a memorial to a bishop. The memorial was in Tewkesbury Cathedral, and had been designed by the bishop himself as a loving bequest to his flock. It depicted the bishop, divested of his gaiters and all other attire, as a stone corpse, recumbent and partly decayed, with snakes crawling out of his eye sockets, a toad squatting between his teeth, a snail on his navel, and moles chewing at the remains of his genitals. It was doubtful as natural history but, as the bishop's last sermon, it had power.

Poe emptied his glass at a gulp.

Mag came back in haste through the curtained doorway, followed by the physician, a paunchy, bearded man of crapulous appearance, his fancy sleeve garters and his shirt dickey disheveled, one hand pawing at his fly buttons, the other arm windmilling to hitch up his trouser suspenders.

"What now?" he said testily. "What the hell's all this about?"

"Derringer went off accidental, Doc," explained the landlord.

"They always do," said the doctor. "Where in thunder are my pince-nez?"

"Right here, Doc," Mag said, "hangin' down your back on this here ribbon."

Restored to his pince-nez, the doctor adjusted it on his nose and, lifting Duprez's dangling arm, felt for his pulse. Poe felt for the bottle. He refilled his glass.

"How about it, Doc?" the landlord asked anxiously.

"H'm," said the doctor. "Pulse is weak—very weak."

"Here's hoping," said Poe.

The landlord rounded on him. "For what?"

"Hope," said Poe gloomily.

He drank, thinking of the waste of that travel document under Duprez's chest as he slumped there over the table with his pulse petering out.

"Come on," said the doctor. "Help me lift him onto the bar there, where I can see the damage. Up with him! Gently, now!"

The doctor and the landlord lifted Duprez and shuffled, grunting, to the bar with him. Mag's voice soared shrilly as she pointed a quivering finger at the table top.

"Look at the blood! Look at the blood!"

The landlord threw a dishrag at her from the bar. "Mop it up, stupid!"

Duprez's removal had disclosed the travel document, and Poe picked it up, explaining to Mag that otherwise blood might get on it. Mag, mopping up, told him that for her part the sight of blood made her heave something fierce.

"Feminine sensitivity," said Poe. "I prescribe a tot for your nausea."

He poured a tot for her, and Mag drank it, and said, "You look kinda peaked, too, mister. You'd best take a slug yourself."

"Considerate as well as sensitive," said Poe. "I'll take your advice."

He did so, and glanced across at the bar, where the doctor was saying, "H'm! The bullet's critically lodged."

"Jesus!" said the landlord. "If he croaks on the prem-ises—"

"He has youth on his side," said the doctor. "I'll need my instruments. He'll do, I guess—when I've extracted the bullet."

"Not here, Doc," pleaded the landlord. "No butchery on the premises!"

"He's well-dressed," said the doctor. "How's he fixed for funds?"

"How would I know, Doc?"

"By going through his pockets. You would later, anyway."

Mag, with the poker, was prodding the bloody dishrag be-tween the bars of the stove.

"There," she said reassuringly to Poe, as the rag began to smolder and stink, "all mopped up."

Poe's eyes were on the landlord, who was showing the doctor a fat wallet from Duprez's pocket.

"Ah, yes," said the doctor. "Quite so. A *good* patient."

"So how about taking him to your place, Doc? We can't have him on the premises, a shot-up person. The goddam con-stables cost too much."

"H'm, well now," said the doctor, with unction, "if I could

find room for him as a resident patient, he'd have the benefit of skilled attention, devoted nursing—''

Poe, meditative, the document in his hand, inquired, ''Your prognosis is hopeful, Doctor?''

''Why, sir,'' replied Dr. Halloran, rumpling up his beard, ''in my professional care, all things being equal, I'll go out on a limb and predict he'll be convalescent in a matter of weeks.''

''That's as good a bet as the U.S. Mint!'' said the landlord, relieved. ''Hey, you, Mag, go find a cab. Get Pat Dooley—he can keep his mouth shut!''

''Now, wait,'' said the doctor. ''Hold your horses, my beer-vending friend. As a medical man, I must report shootings.''

''What, between friends? Hell, Doc, why make trouble?''

The physician drew himself up, a monument to civic rectitude in sleeve garters. ''That gentleman there was a witness. He may feel it his duty, as a responsible citizen—''

''He's fresh in from out of town,'' argued the landlord. ''Doc, have a heart! This here gent don't want to get involved in no shooting case.'' He looked across anxiously at Poe.

Poe, the document in his hand, was seeing in his mind the stage door of a theatre, somewhere in the South, and a man stepping out into the moonlight—a thin man in a black cloak and tall beaver hat, a man who cast a long shadow, a man with a painted face. And what thoughts? That the frail woman he had left in the dressing room, unsuspecting, and the child there asleep in a prop basket would be better off without him? What thoughts, poor tortured mummer, penniless rat, standing there hesitant in the moonlight? Frogs croaked, the crickets seethed. Nocturne for a strolling player. In sudden resolve, he turned and, following his long shadow, walked rapidly away—into Nowhere.

Strange, Poe thought, strange how the patterns of behavior, in any family, tended to repeat themselves in successive generations—father to son. With himself gone, Edgar out of their lives, Mr. Allan would care for Virginia and her mother. . . .

''Right, mister?''

Poe looked up. The landlord, the doctor, the wench Mag were staring at him. He drew in his breath, cast off all doubt. To the analytical mind, logic imposed one inevitable response to every situation. He held the key to his own situation in his hand. He pocketed the document, tossed his cigar stub into the cinder tray and, rising, picked up his West Point greatcoat. As he shrugged into it, the doctor and the landlord and the wench watched him in suspense.

"Hell, mister," warned the landlord, "you go to these here New York constables an' you got trouble. Questions, statements —you could be held—material witness . . ."

Poe picked up his tall hat. He stalked to the street door, jerked back the bolt. His hand on the latch, he turned, a twisted smile under his thin black moustache.

"Behold," he said, "an act of oblivion!"

He lifted the latch. Impelled by the wind, the door burst open with a force that hurled him back. Recovering, he clapped on his hat firmly and, bowing his head to the freezing inrush, stepped out into the turbulent night.

The wind, reeking of the sea, tore at him. Holding on his hat, he looked up at the carven figureheads that leaned and the massive bowsprits that thrust, all uneasily rocking, over the high wooden fence facing him across the street rutted by iron-shod dray wheels and puddled by rain and the stamp of heavy hoofs.

Behind him, the lamplight fanning out from the tavern doorway vanished as the door was forced shut from within. Not a soul was in sight. He was alone.

British ship *Ludgate Hill,* lading for Vigo, Spain.

Which ship?

The surge and tumult of the sea was in his ears, and the gale harped shrill in the masts and yards that soared in swaying ellipses against the sky where moon gleams wanly nimbused the fringes of the cloud scud flying in from the wild Atlantic.

He licked salt from his lips—and stiffened, intently listening, as there began to ring out in ragged unison, far and wide over the city, a thin clangor of bells.

The New Year! His heart gave a great thump. Resolve steeled him. War in Poland! A fresh start or a fair conclusion—for a man best forgotten?

This year would tell.

He began to walk.

Four

Now, in a drugged, uneasy drowse, he lay with closed eyes, vaguely conscious of sweat on his brow and in the palms of his hands, and a dreamlike feeling of vertigo.

He knew it well, this illusion of being lifted, of a long, gentle heave under him, and a slow falling away. He had felt it before, in strange places—railroad depot benches, saloon doorways, back alleys, even police cells.

Drunk again! Where was it this time? Best not open his eyes. Maybe he was in his own bed, and Aunt Maria Clemm would be looking down at him with that expression of uncomplaining martyrdom which was harder to bear than any reproach, and

Virginia, beside her, would giggle, half-amused, half-shocked, "Oh, Eddie! *Again?*"

Her face—so young, so frail in its frame of ringlets—swam dizzily before his eyelids.

He groaned in remorse, murmuring, "I was a child, and she was a child,/In a kingdom by the sea,/But we loved with a love—"

Thin and remote, a cry sounded: "Land ho!"

He stirred restlessly, muttering, "That was more than love,/I and—"

Something thudded heavily on wood, just above his face. His eyes opened—to the blackness of what he sensed to be some narrow, unknown place.

"Virginia?" he called hoarsely.

No answer. He could see nothing. His sight was gone. Bad cigars! He was blind! He raised a hand to his eyes, and the hand struck on wood, covering him. What was this? He groped at the wood with both hands, fumbling, exploring.

Knockings sounded, thuds. Earth clods on a coffin lid? Suddenly it flashed on him what was happening to him. Catalepsy, his lifelong dread! They were burying him alive! Panic seized him.

He screamed, "No! Stop! I'm alive! Alive! *Stop!*"

He strained upward with all his strength at the coffin lid. It was immovable, screwed down securely against the invading worm.

"Help!" he shrieked. "Stop! Oh, God! *Help me!*"

With a rasp of rings, a curtain was swept violently aside. Sunshine flooded dazzlingly into his eyes, a voice was shouting in his ears.

"Alive? Of course you're alive! Good God, man, pull yourself together! You're all right, Mr. Duprez!"

"Daylight?" gasped Poe, unbelieving.

"Daylight indeed, sir, and God's good sunshine!"

Poe became aware of a head talking at him. The head, which was on a level with his own, resembled a billiard ball with eyes and sidewhiskers.

"You're in your cabin, man," said the head, agitated. "You're snoozing in your upper bunk with the curtains drawn!"

"Sir Bartle Mole," Poe croaked.

"Your servant, sir! No pitchfork demon from the Pit! Just your cabin mate. Come now—get that goblin glare out of your eyes! Man alive, what a turn you gave me, thrashing around behind those curtains!"

"My apologies, Sir Bartle," Poe faltered. "I—I was taking a siesta."

"A mistake, Mr. Duprez, a bad habit! I never did hold with afternoon sleeping. It breeds nightmares. Come now, show a leg—come down out of that bunk!"

"No bed of roses," Poe admitted, as he climbed down from it shakily.

"Landfall," said Sir Bartle. "I came below to tell you. Vigo's in sight—nineteen days out from New York, a fast passage. Man, you're all a-twitch. You look ghastly."

"Bronchitis," said Poe, by way of alibi. "I begged laudanum for it from the ship's medicine chest."

"Apothecary's nostrums," snorted Sir Bartle. "Here, this'll do you more good. Try a tot from my flask."

"Willingly," said Poe. He raised the flask in a toast. "To landfall—and Lazarus. I know how he felt!"

Debilitated by the shocks of interment without lilies and exhumation without license, he drank with a thirst that startled Sir Bartle.

"Have a heart, Mr. Duprez—leave me a drop!" Retrieving the flask, Sir Bartle consumed what little was left in it. "*Ah!*" he said, smacking his lips. "Napoleon's own physic. When he captured the Pyramids, he revived the mummies with it—and they'd been embalmed for forty centuries. How're you feeling now?"

"Coming around," said Poe.

Sunshine from the open porthole filled the cramped cabin with a brightness that banished the ghouls of nightmare to mop and mow in their crypts.

From the deck above sounded shouts, thumps, rattlings. Feet tramped, capstan-pawls clanked, block-sheaves squealed. All life was astir, in the briskness of arrival, as the ship moved slowly with a heave to the sea swell.

"So we lose you here, Mr. Duprez," said Sir Bartle, screwing the top back onto his flask. "M'self, I go on to Port o' Bristol. I've got Lady M. and four fine, stout daughters waiting for me—Freda, Frances, Felicity and Flo—my English roses, I call them. They'll be at my little country place, Mole Park, near Winchcombe, wondering if Papa got himself scalped by the Red Indians." He patted his hairless dome. "Yes, a few more days and I'll be back to the Wars of the Roses." He chuckled. "I shall miss your recitations in the saloon, Mr. Duprez."

"Trifles, Sir Bartle," said Poe, adjusting his black cravat before the bulkhead mirror over the tiny fixed washbasin, "—small diversions to mitigate the tedium of the voyage."

"And admirably so," said Sir Bartle. "I take off my hat to flights of fancy. I don't indulge in 'em m'self, of course. As a banker in sound practice, I keep both feet firmly on the ground. But come now—let's get out of this fug and go topside into God's good air. They took the hatches off the hold an hour ago. I saw your trunk hove up."

"Trunk?" Poe's hands, at his cravat, were suddenly still. He looked sharply at Sir Bartle's reflection in the mirror.

"I saw your name painted on it," said the banker, "'Henry Lane Duprez, Passenger to Vigo.' You'd better come topside and keep an eye on it. There'll be Spanish bumboatmen swarming aboard any minute. The Hucksters' Navy, Mr. Duprez—pirates, every man jack of 'em!"

But Poe was thinking about the trunk. Vaguely, now, he recalled some mention of a trunk, by the unfortunate Duprez, back at The Shamrock House tavern on the New York front. Trunk! Duprez had a trunk on board. Poe needed time to digest this information.

"Sir Bartle, I'll sponge the dews of delirium from my face and join you anon."

"See you topside, then," said Sir Bartle, and departed.

Left alone, Poe stepped to the porthole and looked out.

Bright but none too warm, the January sunshine gleamed on the lazy blue swell of the sea. Flashes of white against cliffs still distant, the hue of terra-cotta, marked the toss of breaking waves. Green meadows capped the cliff tops. Above the white walls of a building, small in the distance and solitary on the cliff top, poked up the dark, pointed fingers of cypresses.

Europe! There it was. He was seeing it with his own eyes, through the prism of a thousand books. All its half-familiar unfamiliarity, all the mystery it held for him of other lives and other ways, seemed drawn to a focus there in that cliff-top building, that house with the cypresses, secretive in the January sunlight, above the breaking waves.

The ichor of discovery thrilled in his veins.

Spain of the countless battlefields! To the east somewhere, the Pyrenees and the undying echo of the trumpets of Charlemagne. To the south, where those cliffs reached away into the blue, lay Portugal, land of Camoens of the *Lusiads,* of Marshal Soult at Santarem with the eagles of France, facing Wellington gray-coated and hooknosed on a white horse, on the rolling hills of the Torres Vedras Lines.

Memories of studies at West Point thronged Poe's mind. West Point! What had possessed him, why had he been so mad as to throw away that key to the life he was born to live?

What name had the malicious fiend that rode, spurring, on his back?

He stood for a long time at the porthole, watching Europe tilting nearer toward him over the lift and fall of the sea. Then, tearing himself away from the sight, he opened the cupboard under the diminutive washbasin. Alongside, his tall beaver hat and West Point greatcoat hung from a hook on the bulkhead. He took a ewer from the cupboard, splashed water into the basin.

Europe, yes. But between him and the war in Poland stretched a long, long road. First call—Paris—and the Lafayette Circle. But it was a long road, too, even to Paris, for an adventurer with a dollar in his pocket. The fare in public diligences, from staging post to staging post, cost money. On the other hand. . . .

Poe looked at his reflection in the bulkhead mirror.

"Dialogue," he said to it, "between the Devil and Conscience. The Devil: Henry Lane Duprez has a trunk on board— and *you* are Duprez! Conscience: You're nothing of the kind— you're Edgar Poe and that trunk and its contents are not your property. The Devil: Duprez's dead—it's a dead man's property —what can *he* do with it? Conscience: What can *you*, Edgar Poe? The Devil: Pawn the lot!"

He plunged his hands into the basin and, bending over it, dashed water into his face.

Through the porthole came a sound of distant shouting.

Poe, hands in the basin, lifted his face, water dripping from his hair and moustache, to stare at his reflection in the mirror.

He said to it: "Conscience: Duprez may live—to claim his trunk. The Devil: So, then, craven, go walk! Go *beg* your way to Paris! Where's your pride?"

Poe took a towel from a bulkhead hook. The confused sound of shouting was growing louder. Drying his face, he stepped to the porthole and looked out.

A rabble of small craft had hove in sight. Here came Spain! The circle of the porthole framed the oncoming bumboats, vying with each other to reach the ship, gliding slowly under shortened sail. Oars dipped and rose, flashing in the sunshine. Swarthy men in tatters and gaudy head bandannas were standing, yelling, in the bows of the boats, which held piles of oranges and lemons. The standing men brandished demijohns, ornate shawls, mantillas of black and white lace, Cordoba hats, beribboned tambourines and banderillas. The Hucksters' Navy!

Shouts came strident across the water: *"Hola! Bienvenidos! Hay frutas! Hay vino! Hay trajes tipicos! Barato! Todo barato, caballeros!"*

Poe watched the bumboat fleet come huddling alongside. The hucksters began hurling up oranges, lemons, rolls of twine with one end tied to demijohns, to passengers on the deck above.

"Naranjas!" screeched the hucksters. *"Frutas frescas! Limones!"*

Poe turned back to the mirror, threw the towel aside, smoothed back with his hands the wet, thinning hair from his prominent brow.

He said to the mirror: "Conscience: You've borrowed a man's name, but you need it no longer, so why walk in his shoes? The Devil: You are off to the wars—so dress for it!"

The hubbub of the hucksters mingled with the din on the deck above as Poe faced rigidly in the mirror the stare of his own eyes, hectic with challenge.

"Soldier of fortune?" demanded the man in the mirror. "Returning some day from the wars, triumphant—with the plunder of Muscovy?"

Poe stared at the challenger—and in sudden, hard decision nodded his acquiescence.

He snatched his hat from the hook and, the question answered, left the cabin, not seeing the object which sailed in through the porthole and fell with a splash into the basin. It was a lemon.

"Open up," said the little old stooped man in the carpet slippers, the black alpaca suit, and the beret, as he combed his gray wisp of goatee with yellow fingernails.

But Poe looked uneasily at the trunk on the counter—the leather trunk, tight-strapped, with the name DUPREZ printed on it in white paint.

What did he really know about Duprez, bloodily struck down in that far-off tavern? A stranger's trunk! Who could divine what it might conceal, what object of passion or token of revenge? Strange, the suggestive power of a stranger's trunk, Poe reflected, gazing at it, imagining himself starting back, aghast, from the revelation of a severed head, a gliding viper, or a venomous tarantula.

"*Por favor!*" begged the little old man. Impatient, he pulled his beret about on his head, hanks of gray hair drooping about his ears. "*Vamos, caballero!*"

Around Poe, here in the Monte de Piedad, the Mount of Pity—otherwise, the Vigo pawnshop—loomed stacks of musty clothing, flyblown pier glasses, funereal paintings, plaster Virgins in faded finery, clocks without hands and jugs without handles, a brass-topped coffee table on a support of crossed shinbones, a moulting bull's head with glass eyes bulging and one ear amputated, a stuffed wildcat with tiger stripes and needle-sharp, snarling fangs.

From outside the iron grill of the grimy window came a wailing cry: "*Basura! Basura!*" In the alley where the sunset was fading, a man plodded by, leading a mule panniered with reeking garbage sacks. The mule's dainty hoofs clinked on the cobbles. "*Basura! Basura!*" The nasal ululation faded into the distance.

"*Caballero,*" pleaded the little old pawnbroker, drywashing his hands.

Annoyed with literary habits of thought now abandoned for the path of action, Poe unbuckled the straps of the trunk, threw back the lid. Clothing was neatly folded in the trunk. On top of the clothing lay a box of cigars, a well-worn little red-leather case, and a miniature in an oval frame.

The pawnbroker's avid hands delved into the trunk, but Poe pushed them away.

"All in good time, my friend!"

He picked up the miniature. A fair-haired girl, gray-eyed,

smiling—Duprez's English girl undoubtedly, his lost love, Kate something—Castle, Caswell? In any event, the miniature obviously had sentimental value. It was not a thing that a gentleman and an officer—or officer-to-be on reaching Poland, and certainly an ex-cadet of West Point—would lightly pawn, however reduced his circumstances.

"Not this," he said, pocketing the miniature in his greatcoat.

He opened the red-leather case. It contained collar studs, cufflinks, a gold half-hunter watch with a jeweled fob, a little ring box. There was engraving on the back of the watch case.

The pawnbroker reached for it, but Poe, reading the engraved lettering, said, "No! This is a presentation watch."

It was a gift to Henry Lane Duprez from his father—a twenty-first birthday gift. The gracious life, Poe mused, envisioning the Duprez plantation, the white-pillared façade of the mansion, the celebrations for the son-and-heir's majority; elegant young gallants and hoop-skirted belles gossiping on the lawns, while faithful Negro slaves, wreathed in smiles, circulated deferentially from group to group with trays of mint juleps. Ah, home! Poe sighed, nostalgic.

"Not this," he said, pocketing the watch.

He opened the little ring box. A diamond solitaire flashed in the waning light from the window as Poe took the ring from the box.

"A fair stone, *caballero*," conceded the pawnbroker, licking his lips.

But written on the inside of the band, engraved in the gold in tiny lettering, were the names "Kate" and "Henry."

"Not this!" Poe returned the ring to its blue-velvet slot, pocketed the box. "Engagement ring," he explained.

The pawnbroker, in exasperation, clutched his beret in both hands, lifted it straight up into the air, muttered imprecations at it, then returned it to his head. "*Señor!*" he protested.

But Poe was adamant. Who knew? One day, God willing, he

might be able to return these particular articles anonymously to Henry Lane Duprez of New Orleans, should he learn that the young tobacco planter's constitution had prevailed over the surgical assistance of Dr. Halloran.

"You can value the studs and cufflinks," Poe graciously told the pawnbroker. "I carry letters of credit drawn on bankers of consequence in Paris, but until I reach there to encash them I find myself, amusingly enough, embarrassed for immediate funds." He smiled to show how amused he was at his quaint predicament. "An unlucky run with the cards, you know, during the Atlantic crossing." He shrugged carelessly. "Easy come, easy go."

"Paris?" said the pawnbroker. He shuffled his carpet slippers to the window and prodded with a horny fingernail at the links and studs in the case, to catch the light on them. "A long, cold journey to Paris, *caballero!*" Winter in the Pyrenean passes—"

"No doubt," Poe agreed. "I shall need, then, to keep some of this warm clothing from my trunk. I'll pick out what I want and you can value the rest."

He chose what he needed from the trunk, finding no great reason to carp at Duprez's sartorial taste, and looked around over the Mount of Pity's junk heaps to see if there was anything that might be of use to him on a journey that could perchance prove arduous.

Umbrella handles and sword hilts protruded from the mouth of a cracked amphora. He took out one of the swords, thinking it not beyond the bounds of possibility that he might encounter brigands lurking around the mountain passes.

He made to sweep the sword out from its scabbard, but the blade was not easily sweepable, being rusted in. He exerted his strength, which made him cough, but the blade emerged with a reluctant rasping.

"Ah, that!" said the pawnbroker. "A fine weapon, sir— *espada de matador!* It belonged to Niño de La Puebla, of this

parish—God rest his soul," added the pawnbroker, crossing himself. "See there, that bull's head! A very great bull—six hundred and seventy-five kilos. Such horns! They did Niño de La
Puebla's business for him at the Fair of San Ignacio. Mark
them and tremble!"

But Poe rapped, "On guard!" and with the sword made a
thrust or two at the bull's head. Ye gods, how vividly the heft
of a weapon in his hand again brought back the old days at
West Point!

"A bargain, *caballero!*" enthused the usurer. "Sword and
head for a hundred *reales!* They are choice—they have asso-
ciations!"

Poe tried an attack *en tierce* at the wildcat, snarling man-
gily at him from where it crouched on a pedestal.

"I was trained," Poe said, panting a little, "to a heavier
weapon—the cut-and-slash of the cavalry saber."

"Forty *reales* for the sword," said the pawnbroker, de-
ferring to criticism. He pulled his beret about hopefully on his
head. "A fine Toledo blade!"

"I'll take it," said Poe, "—for a toothpick."

Breathing hard from his exertions, he caught sight of his
multiple reflections in the flyspecked, gilt-framed pier glasses.
Seeing himself thus, in caped West Point greatcoat and tall
beaver hat, sword in hand, he felt again a surge of expectation
and confidence. He had burned his boats. He must go forward
or perish. He could shed his alias, be at last his own man, a free
man—Edgar Poe; filibuster, roaming mercenary with a sword
for hire; the world a cannonball at his feet.

He saluted his martial reflections with the sword.

"*Nada mas!*" bawled the coachman, reining in his plodding
team. "*Nada mas allà, por Dios!*"

Snowflakes whirling out of the darkness turned gray in the
light which glowed dimly from the snow-caked windows of a
single-story building squatted in a white drift. The diligence

trundled heavily to a standstill and, stiff, dazed, half-frozen, travelers stumbled out: a fat French silk merchant from Lyons, three surly and uncommunicative nondescripts, and a soldier of fortune in a tall hat, with ice beads in his moustache.

From the low eaves of the building, cowled in white, hung a wind-rocked signboard, snow-clotted and unreadable, but the driver of the diligence, a snowman pixie-capped in a tarred sack, clambered down from his box and with a wave of his arm made the five huddled travelers free of the building.

"Fonda de la Concepción, *señores. Hay camas!*"

"Beds?" said Poe. "We spend the night here?"

"Mayhap many nights," said the coachman. "There's drifts here in the foothills. It'll be worse, up in the pass. I go no farther in this weather."

He turned to unharness his team. Poe, carrying the carpet bag and umbrella he had purchased at the Vigo Monte de Piedad, regretted that Duprez's shoes had not fitted him. There was a hole in the right sole of his own, and he could feel snow leaking wetly through it as he accompanied his fellow travelers into the inn.

Its warm fug embraced them as, with eyes dazzled by lamp-light, they stood stamping their feet on the brick floor, shaking snow from their garments, removing gloves to blow on nails blue with cold.

Poe had lost count of time since he had set out from Vigo, but each night on this interminable journey to the Spanish frontier the accommodations had grown more primitive.

Here in this one-roomed barn of a *fonda,* a ladder at one end slanted up to a loft where truckle beds were visible in the lamplight. At the other end, peat hags smoldered, banking a blaze of logs on the hearth under the wide, smoke-blackened chimney arch. Four elderly men, peasants, sitting on benches around the fire, turned the clay pipes they were sucking at for a look at the travelers; and at a massive, scarred table a stout woman with a moustache held a bloody chopper poised over a pale, shaven shoat with modestly lowered eyelashes and an innocent smile.

"*Buenas noches, señores,*" said the stout woman, and brought down the chopper with a bang on the table, neatly bisecting the piglet's smile.

From low beams hung bundles of garlic, onions, *chorizo* sausages, snow-cured hams, dripping goat curds maturing in cheesecloth. All added their olfactory mite to the cozy fug, which was principally contributed to by the steam from the cauldron bubbling over the blaze on the hearth, the sharpness of mulling cider and of *vinto tinto* from the drip pans under the casks trestled around the walls.

The peasants around the fire made room for the travelers to warm themselves. The coachman of the diligence came stamping in, roaring his complaints of the weather. The stout hostess clopped about in her clogs and black woollen stockings. She removed the piglet from the table, mopped up the blood with her apron, hacked maize bread from a cartwheel-sized loaf that leaned against the wall. She distributed doorstep slices around the table, with a spoon, a knife, and a horn bowl and mug to each place. She drew a jug of wine from a cask, then with a curved poker unhooked the cauldron and, tottering under its weight, carried it steaming to the table.

"*Comida,*" she informed the travelers and the coachman.

They sat down on the benches that flanked the table. The hostess ladled out the soup liberally. The peasants stayed around the fire, sucking at their pipes. They had evidently dined. They passed a *bota,* a wineskin, from one to another, each toasting the travelers with Spanish peasant courtesy, "*Buen' provecha, señores!*"

It was good soup. Warmed by it and by copious draughts of the wine, Poe expanded. He surveyed his fellow travelers, greedily spooning, munching and quaffing.

"*Buen' provecha,*" he said. "The time-honored term—

'Good appetite!'—occurs frequently in your own classic, *Don Quijote de la Mancha,* which I've had the pleasure of reading, with the aid of sundry dictionaries, in the original.''

The travelers went on spooning and slobbering, but the peasants nodded their courteous interest at Poe and said *"Claro!"* to each other. The hostess was frying huge chops in a great black pan, prodding at them with a fork as long as her fat arm.

Poe finished his soup, looked into the cauldron and, finding it empty, refilled his mug from the wine jug. He noticed the peasants watching him, evidently in hopes of some further pregnant observation from him. With a renewed sense of the magic of finding himself here in authentic Spain, he obliged them.

"Your immortal Cervantes," he remarked, "whom I venture to think of as a friend and colleague, has in his great work a passage fortuitously apt to our present surroundings. It goes somewhat to this effect: 'Sancho, we are come to an inn. Maybe the goodwife will find a pair of fat cockerels to simmer for us in her pot, then honest fellowship and good appetite—*buen' prove-cha!*—will do the rest.' "

'Claro," nodded the peasants, looking with interest at the learned gentleman who had come among them.

The hostess brought the pan of chops sizzling to the table and forked them out onto the doorsteps of bread, pouring a fair share of the delicious hot fat over each.

The chops were very large. Silence fell during their consumption. There was only the clopping of the hostess's clogs, the hiss of snowflakes falling down the chimney into the fire, the smacking of lips.

Finishing his chop, Poe tossed the bone over his shoulder, where it was deftly caught and crunched by one of the three pointer dogs lurking around hopefully. Poe wiped his fingers with his handkerchief, dabbed it to his moustache, declined the additional chop proffered to him on the hostess's fork. Rising from the bench, he went to his greatcoat, hanging on a hook with his belt and sword. From the deep pocket he took out the box of cigars he had found in Duprez's trunk.

Already he had made considerable inroads on them, but, replete with food and mellowed by wine, he passed the box around to all present—only to find it, when his own turn came, empty. Closing the box, he remarked—with the tactful object of diverting the company's attention from the mischance of his deprivation, which might embarrass them—that it well could be that he had, just now, misquoted the passage from their incomparable Cervantes.

"Memory," he explained, exploring his vest pockets hopefully with a finger and thumb, "can be capricious, though it is, of course, one of mankind's richest gifts."

His finger and thumb encountered a half-smoked cigar. Relieved, he took it from his vest pocket—only to remember, abruptly, from whose lax fingers, in a tavern far distant from this one, it had fallen.

He felt a shadow pass over him.

"Yet, nevertheless," he admitted, shaking his head, "memory can be also, at times, man's heaviest cross."

"*Claro,*" said the peasants, puffing at their cigars—and, impressed by the profundity of the stranger with the big forehead, they nodded sagely at each other.

Overcoming compunction, and with a hand held to conceal the half-smoked condition of the cigar, Poe puffed it alight at one of the lamps.

The travelers, full-fed, joined the peasants around the fire, and one of them urged his wineskin upon Poe.

"*Anis, señor*—the good *aguardiente* of the Widow Chinchon."

He showed Poe how to squeeze a needle-thin jet from the teat without touching the nipple to the mouth—a matter of etiquette which Poe, adept in the various techniques of imbibing, from a goblet of Falernian to a crock of Tennessee moonshine, readily mastered. Reinforced by food, wine and *anis,* he asked the coachman if there was no chance of the journey being continued on the morrow.

"Nobody crosses the pass in this weather," said the coachman.

"*Vamos, hombre!*" said the hostess, busily clanking the pump handle over the brick sink in the corner. "What of the *contrabandistas?* This is weather they pray for. It keeps the *guardias* indoors with their wives—or somebody else's!"

"*Claro!*" cackled the old peasants, slapping their thighs, for evidently they liked to keep in with her.

"If I could reach the railhead over in France," mused the French silk merchant, "I'd be in bed with my own wife, in Lyons, two nights hence."

"A railhead?" Poe exclaimed. The thought, Press on! Press on! buzzed in his mind, with memories of Wellington leading his army over these same mountains, Hannibal surmounting the Alps with elephants, Napoleon burning the Kremlin in the snow. "Sir," he said, "if we can get horses here, we'll ride on together, shoulder to shoulder!"

"Not I," said the merchant, with typical bourgeois sloth. "I'm staying snug here till the diligence leaves."

"I've a horse to sell," said the hostess. She turned, blowing back her moustache and wiping her hands on her bloody apron. "*Ay,* and I'll throw in a saddle with saddlebags, too!"

She appealed to the aged peasants as to the excellence of her horse, and they nodded unanimous corroboration at the soldier of fortune.

"*Claro,*" said the peasants.

Five

As horses go, it was not a bad horse, but now it had gone
more than far enough for one day. Its head hanging, fetlock-
deep in blown snow that had clogged and frozen in its shoes, it
plodded on wearily, up the interminable slope.

Slumped in the saddle, Poe rode with his chin sunk in his
greatcoat, the crown of his hat pressed to the underside of the
umbrella which afforded him some protection from the bite of
the snowflakes wind-driven from the north down the mountain
pass.

Bone-tired, numbed, he was only dimly conscious of the
forested slopes that swept away up, each side of him, to the
Pyrenean summits above timberline.

The umbrella clutched in his gloved hand was heavy with

snow, the capes of his greatcoat were caked with it. Occasional lulls in the rush of the wind roused him to fitful awareness of his own dry coughing, of the muffled thud of the horse's hoofs, of the gurgle of the stream racing down to the right of the trail and narrowed now to a thin black ribbon by the snow-covered sheet ice growing out from the banks.

He rode blind, trusting to the horse.

He had been told the truth about the *guardias*—for, setting out from the Fonda de la Concepción into the howling wilderness at the first gray premonition of the dawn, he had seen all day no *guardia*, in fact no living soul.

Now, slack in the saddle and nodding limply into the shelter of the umbrella, the afternoon drawing in and his breakfast of maize bread broken into a bowl of lumpy hot chocolate not even a beautiful memory, he began to mutter into his greatcoat.

"By a route obscure and lonely,/Haunted by ill angels only,/Where an Eidolon, named Night,/On a black throne reigns upright—"

In a lull of the wind bludgeoning and jerking at his umbrella, a sound reached him—a new sound, different from the dull plodding of the horse and the rush and gurgle of the black, foam-stippled stream.

He raised his head, his stovepipe hat jammed down hard over his prominent temples, and listened. Snowflakes drove at him over the rim of the umbrella. They clung to his eyebrows, his lashes, his moustache, his corpse-pale, stubbled cheeks.

From far off, and high on the white slopes under the gun-metal sky, came the sound again, carried on the moan of the wind—the sound of a thin, long-drawn howl.

He thought of his sword, belted around his middle under his greatcoat. From another quarter came an answering howl, long-drawn, desolate and foreboding.

"K'ck, k'ck," he clicked at his horse, jerking the bridle; and as the horse plodded on up the unending slope, Poe bent his head again to the shelter of the umbrella.

He began to sag once more into a vague, numbed half sleep,

muttering: "I have reached these lands but newly,/Found this ultimate dim Thule—"

A rock pine loomed by, cowled in snow.

"Where the traveler meets, aghast,/Sheeted memories of the past,/Shrouded forms that start and sigh,/As they pass the wanderer by."

He lapsed into a kind of trance, blank and lost, from which he was rudely aroused when the horse suddenly shied, almost unseating him.

He heard a clanking of chains through the grieving wind, and raised his head to peer with narrowed eyes over the rim of his umbrella.

What had made the horse shy was a gallows upstanding from a cairn of stones. Hanging in chains from the gallows, the body of a man swayed and twirled in the wind.

Dazed, swept by the speeding flakes, Poe peered about him. He had lost the stream. He had reached the brow of the pass. A long white slope fell endlessly away in the direction from which he had come, another in the direction in which he was bound.

He looked up at the dangling body. It swayed like a pendulum, this body ripe for the Pit, across a board nailed to the gallows post. The gray daylight was fading rapidly now. He clicked at his horse, heeling it forward, closer to the cairn, so that he could read the notice board.

A skull-and-crossbones, painted in red, grinned down at him.

Beneath it was the warning, crudely lettered:

CONTRABANDISTAS

A LA MUERTE

"Death to smugglers," Poe muttered.

Swaying, clanking, twirling, the hanged man made the horse shy again. Poe lost his grip on his umbrella, and the wind seized it, whirled it up, dropped it, and it went awheeling away wildly like a hoop down the slope up which he had toiled. Sudden rage rose in him.

"Barbarism! Barbarism!" he shouted.

He groped inside his greatcoat for his sword. His numb gloved hand clenched on the hilt. He drew the blade, rasping.

"Fanatics!" he shouted. "Vile inquisitors! Barbarous dons!"

Brandishing his sword, he forced his horse closer to the cairn. He slashed furiously at the chains from which the body dangled, but its gyrations in the wind made him miss, and his sword was up for the cavalry clash, backhand as advocated at West Point, when he heard a shout.

Unbelieving, he saw a man step out from behind the cairn—a man of great stature, silhouetted blackly, in a fisherman's oil-skins and sou'wester, against the snow slope that swept away up behind him to a near summit.

The man shook his head.

"No, 'bor!" he called to Poe. "Sheathe your blade! You'll never get him down that way!"

"An Englishman?" Poe said, incredulous.

"Aye, sir." The big man came around the cairn, gripped the bridle of Poe's horse, made restless by the swaying and clanking and slashing, and turned up to Poe a leathery face, black-bearded and broken-nosed. "You, too, I take it—from that shouting I heard."

"I'm an American," Poe said.

"Nonetheless, welcome to ye!" The man in oilskins led Poe on his horse, sword in hand, around the cairn to the lee side. "And welcome to my camp—if ye've no objection to sharing a gypsy's fire."

"Gypsy?"

"Blood brother to the Romanies, 'bor!"

In the lee of the cairn, where the snow was thin on the ground, stood a small handcart tilted down on its shafts, its contents covered with a tarpaulin. Over a stick fire, redly crackling, a black pot hung, bubbling, from an iron tripod.

"Dismount and eat," said the man in oilskins.

Poe sheathed his sword. So stiff that he scarcely could heave his leg over the saddle, he dismounted.

The man in oilskins fed sticks to the fire. Sparks flew in the deepening darkness. He lifted the lid of the pot, prodded the contents with an iron ladle. The steam of herbs, onions and gamy meat simmering savorily together made Poe's nostrils distend and his belly rumble.

The man in oilskins gestured with the ladle at a white-furred skin, red-gashed by paunching, lying on the snow.

"Mountain hare," he said. He stirred the stew in the pot. "Good enough for a smuggler's dinner."

"Smuggler?"

"Aye, sir."

Daylight was gone, the wind moaned, occasionally snow-flakes eddied grayly in the firelight that ruddied the hardbitten face of the man in oilskins as he stooped over the pot.

"Ye cried out against the dons for inquisitors and fanatics. Ye did well there. What I smuggle," said the man in oilskins, "is proscribed in their Peninsula. So the *guardias,* at the behest of the tonsured brethren, confiscate my wares and throw me out over the border. But I restock—and return by another way. The frontier don't exist, 'bor, that can keep out the love of God—and His True Word."

He peeled back a corner of the tarpaulin corded down over his handcart, and disclosed the contents.

"They look," Poe said, "like—like Bibles!"

"Bibles they are, 'bor," said the man in oilskins. "Bibles for Spain! New Testaments, in the Authorized Version—untampered with by Popery, Mr. American."

"Poe—Edgar A. Poe—sometime of Richmond, Virginia."

"Borrow—George Borrow, of Oulton Broad, in the County of Norfolk—agent for the British and Foreign Bible Society." He dipped out stew from the pot, handed the ladle to Poe. "Taste this."

Poe's numbed hand shook as he took the ladle. The wind

gusted, moaning about the gallows, and the dangling body swayed with a clank of chains.

"Don't let our friend there worry you," said the smuggler. "See, now—he'll help keep us warm this night."

He plucked a burning branch from the fire, clambered up heavy-booted onto the cairn. He seized the hanging body by a leg, thrust the flame up its crotch and held it there. Smoke from damp straw began to leak from the interstices of the body's clothing.

"That'll do it," said Borrow, and he scrambled down from the cairn, loose stones cascading with him.

The blizzard thickened, the flakes swirled by faster. Far off, in the surrounding night faintly luminous from the snow fields, a wolf howled.

Suddenly, with a *whooof*, the dangling effigy burst into flame and, gyrating in the wind, blazed and kicked and twirled wildly on the gallows.

"So much for threats," said the man in oilskins. He thrust the burning branch back under the pot. "How goes the stew, 'bor? Is she ready?"

"Ready," said Poe. "And you save my life with it!"

"Draw in, then. Eat. For food is good," said God's smuggler. "Life is sweet, brother—and there's likewise a wind on the heath."

Six

"Beignets!" cried the doughnut-seller, in a shrill soprano. *"Beignets tout chauds! Ici les beignets véritables!"*

Rings of batter sizzled on the griddle over the charcoal brazier in her barrow in the Rue du Cloître Notre Dame, at the side of the great cathedral.

She stamped her wooden-clogged feet on the cobbles, for the day was freezing cold.

Nearby, two worn stone steps led up to a small iron-studded door in the towering gray stone wall of the cathedral. The steps were white with frost. The door stood open, and just inside it, at the foot of more worn stone steps curving upward into darkness, an aged nun sat on a stool at a small table. Her blue habit was girdled with a white cord, her mittened hands fingered the beads of her rosary, a wide-winged starched wimple framed her furrowed face.

"*Beignets à la liqueur,*" chanted the doughnut-seller, sprinkling drops from a bottle over the bubbling batter. "*Beignets de Notre-Dame—tout chauds, tout chauds!*"

Hoofs rang on cobbles, wheels ground, and from the wide square before the façade of the cathedral, a *fiacre* turned into the narrow Rue du Cloître. The driver, his woolen cap pulled well down over his ears, reined his horse, jingling, blowing steam from flared nostrils, to a halt and flourished his whip at the doorway with the steps.

"*Voilà, m'sieu, -'dame!*"

A short, stout man, side-whiskered, ulstered, silk-hatted, stepped out of the fiacre and turned to give a hand to a girl to alight.

In coat and hat of fur, her hands in a muff, she tilted her bright face to look up at the gargoyles which protruded their reptilian snouts from the leads of the cathedral roof high up under the goose-gray clouds.

"The view is famous," she said. "No visitor to Paris should miss it, of course. But are you sure you're equal to the climb, Sir Bartle?"

"A mere pipe-opener, Miss Eleanor," Sir Bartle Mole assured her gallantly, muttering to himself as he paid the cabman. "Damme, I once mounted a duchess!"

"*Beignets!*" chanted the doughnut-seller. "*Goûtez mes beignets, m'sieu -'dame!*"

Sir Bartle tossed her a coin, which she caught in her apron. The fiacre trundled off jingling. Sir Bartle dropped another coin into the offertory plate on the nun's table and, following his attractive young companion, started to mount the staircase that spiraled upward, in this one of the cathedral's twin towers, to the roof.

Daylight from the doorway faded as he mounted. The stone

staircase grew narrower between cold stone walls. Soon it was pitch dark, and the soprano cry of the doughnut-seller below sounded thin and remote.

Sir Bartle began to breathe stertorously as he toiled on upward, fumbling with the guide rope slung between iron rings on the wall to his right.

Eleanor's voice floated down to him hollowly from the darkness above: "Are you all right, Sir Bartle?"

"Coming, m'dear," he panted bravely, and toiled on upward, muttering, "I deserve the Garter for this!"

Wan daylight appeared on a curve above him. The daylight came from a rusty-barred window slit, the panes leaded and spider-webbed, on his left. Sir Bartle paused by the window to remove his hat and mop perspiration from his flushed bald head. He felt for his snuffbox, sniffed up a pinch in each nostril, and sneezed healthily. It relieved his pounding temples.

"Miss Eleanor?" he called, into the darkness above. "How much farther?"

"Not far now," her voice floated down ghostly to him. "Courage, Sir Bartle!"

"Courage, she says," muttered the banker. "These American petticoats! Worse than my four English roses—and I'll be lucky if I survive to see *them* again." He toiled on upward into the dark, mumbling, "Nearer, my God, to Thee—by way of a thundering apoplexy, like as not!"

A deafening iron clangor shook the blackness, wringing from him an appalled shout: "Good grief—the Last Trump!"

Through vibrant, deep, dying reverberations, Eleanor's voice floated down, excited: "The bell! The great *Bourdon* in the other tower, Sir Bartle! Do hurry! The bells are going to ring!"

The carillon was indeed pealing as Sir Bartle tottered at last, by way of a narrow door, onto the leads under the gray sky.

"Are you all right?" Eleanor asked, concerned. "Your face looks all purple!"

But Sir Bartle, open-mouthed, hat in one hand, handkerchief in the other, stood staring.

The leads of the roof stretched away before him. To the right was the pillared parapet high above the great square. To the left the leads sloped steeply upward to a higher level of the roof where the dome swelled. Scattered about on the leads were the watchful guardians of Paris, frozen in stone—hellhounds, chimeras, werewolves, creatures with the leering heads of satyrs and the bodies of winged cats. A forest of gargoyles, and there among them a solitary man—a man in black, his beaver hat tall against the sky as he stood with black-gloved hands on the parapet and, gazing out over the widespread expanse of roof-tops and smoking chimney pots, declaiming through the clangor of the carillon:

"—of the bells—iron bells! What a world of solemn thought their melody compels!"

"Good heavens alive!" said Sir Bartle in recognition and stupefaction.

"That man's reciting," said Eleanor in wonder.

"He's apt to, at times," explained Sir Bartle.

Bing—bang—bong! rang the carillon as Poe, unaware that he was observed, flung out his gloved hand, with a hole in the right forefinger, at the incomparable vista that inspired him.

"And the people—ah, the people—/They that dwell up in the steeple/All alone—"

BONG! went the great bell, the *Bourdon.*

"Ah, their King it is who tolls," proclaimed Poe, "And he rolls, rolls, rolls/ A paean from the bells!"

Bing—bang—bong!

BONG!

Eleanor and Sir Bartle, he with his hat in his hand and his handkerchief to his brow, stood rooted in fascination as Poe exulted:

"And his merry bosom swells/ With the clamor of the bells—"

Carried away by the iron din, transported, he broke into a

kind of dance, a curious cross between a fandango and a horn-pipe, pulling at imaginary ropes, proclaiming:

"And he dances, and he yells,/ Keeping time, time, time,/ In a sort of Runic rhyme,/ To the paean of the bells—"

Bing—bang—bong!

BONG! from the giant *Bourdon*.

"Of the bells, bells, bells,/ To the throbbing of the bells,/ To the sobbing of the bells,/ To the rolling and the tolling of the bells, bells, bells—"

Bing—bang—bong! pealed the carillon.

BONG! thundered the *Bourdon*.

"To the moaning," gasped Poe, "and the groaning—of the bells—"

All in, coughing from his exertions, he sagged against his greatcoat, which was folded over the parapet, as the iron clangor fell silent, save for its vibrations humming on the air here, high above Paris.

"*Mr. Duprez!*" Sir Bartle clapped on his hat and, followed by Eleanor, who was highly intrigued, walked forward to Poe. "Good heavens, sir, what a performance!"

Poe turned quickly, in shock, his handkerchief to his moustache.

"Well, well! It's a small world, Mr. Duprez," said Sir Bartle. "Eleanor, allow me to present a compatriot of yours—"Mr. Henry Lane Duprez, of New Orleans. Miss Eleanor Gerrard from North Carolina."

Conscious of a possible unconventionality in his behavior, and embarrassed at detection in it by a young lady of elegance and charm, Poe held his hat to his chest with one hand, inconspicuously clenched the other to conceal the hole in his glove, and bowed deeply.

"Miss Gerrard," he said, "what must you think of me? Cavorting, as it were, among these Gothic grotesques!"

"Oh, but you enhanced their effect delightfully, Mr. Duprez," Eleanor assured him, her blue eyes dancing.

"We wouldn't have missed it for the world, would we, Sir Bartle?"

"Humph," said the banker doubtfully.

Poe explained, "I reached Paris after dark last night, and this morning I climbed to this hallowed roof for my first view of the city."

"Every visitor should, of course," Eleanor agreed.

"Frankly," Poe said, "I thought myself alone—and I fear that the splendor of the prospect, here spread before us, overcame my decorum."

"And no wonder!" Eleanor moved to the parapet to feast her eyes on the prospect. "What person of spirit could fail to be inspired by it?"

"Unfortunately," said Poe, "it's a failing inherent in human nature that its sincere response to the sublime can all too often appear little short of ridiculous." Thinking it politic to change the subject, he pointed. "Yonder on that eminence stands Napoleon's Arc de Triomphe. Building started on the morrow of Austerlitz, and is just now completed in this reign of Louis-Philippe."

"Magnificent," said Eleanor.

From far below, in the great square before the cathedral, rose a multifarious clatter of horses' hoofs. Poe leaned over the parapet, looking down, and his eyes kindled at the sight of cavalry, dwarfed there below, crossing the square toward the river which, bearing patches of ice on its current, flowed slowly under the gray stone bridges.

"A squadron of hussars," said Poe, "—hussars of Conflans, I fancy."

Spokes of sunshine, penetrating the cloud, gilded a dome on the left bank of the Seine.

"The dome of the Invalides," said Poe, "—asylum for veterans of the wars, and headquarters of the War Ministry."

"The cannons in the courtyard," said Eleanor, "look like a child's toys."

"Indeed yes, from our present elevation, but I believe they're still fired on state occasions. It's a saluting battery—the fourteen cannons and four mortars of Napoleon's own *batterie triomphale*."

Eleanor, glancing sidelong at him curiously, laid a slim gloved hand on his greatcoat, folded over the parapet.

"You are of a military bent," she said, "and this, unless I'm much mistaken, is a West Point greatcoat."

Poe bowed acquiescence, with a modest gesture, and turned to the banker.

"But, Sir Bartle—when I took leave of you at Vigo, you were Bristol-bound."

"On arriving home," said Sir Bartle, "to the embraces of Lady M. and my four English roses, I found a letter awaiting me there. It was from Miss Gerrard's father, who was a kind host to me in America. He told me that Eleanor, in her travels, would be visiting Paris, so I hurried straight over here by the Channel packet. I'm determined to take her home for a stay at Mole Park. Lady M. will adore her, and I'm sure she'll find much in common with my daughters—Freda, Frances, Felicity and Flo."

"I can just picture them, Sir Bartle," said Eleanor, "and I look upon the visit as a treat in store, though I fear you'll have to *drag* me away from Paris! And you, Mr. Duprez— you've arrived to take up an appointment, maybe, as military attaché at our Embassy here?"

"Not," Poe admitted, "exactly. In fact, my plans depend— more or less—on my finding the headquarters here of a Franco-American association known as the Lafayette Circle."

"Oh, how lucky we met!" Eleanor exclaimed. "*I* can take you there!"

"Indeed?" Poe's heart soared.

Eleanor said, "I have a letter to deliver to Colonel Sauvagnac, who presides over the Paris chapter of the Circle. He's an intimate friend of my father's, Mr. Duprez."

"Indeed?" said Poe, again. But his heart sank.

Duprez! Eleanor and Sir Bartle were hoisting him again with his borrowed name. He was in a predicament.

This was by no means the first time that the logic of circumstance had obliged him to use names not his own. There was a certain tobacconist whose bill had been returned marked "Addressee Unknown." But that was long ago, and it was a rare addict who could claim that he never had perpetrated some trifling delinquency in order to relish the embraces of the Lady Nicotine. In any case, the matter of the tobacconist had borne highly comical fruit in the shape of an essay entitled "Diddling Considered as One of the Exact Sciences."

Less diverting in its results had been his impetuous enlistment in the ranks of the U.S. Army under the name of Edgar A. Perley. Military-minded as he was, he had discovered that noncommissioned rank was uncongenial, in that it lacked scope, and he had prevailed on his foster father, wealthy Mr. Allan, not only to buy him out but to give him one last chance. Conditional on it being irrevocably the last, Mr. Allan had used his influence with a certain senator to nominate Poe for a West Point cadetship, which had eventuated—but of which, Poe had to admit to himself, full advantage had not been taken.

Often as he had regretted this, never had he done so more poignantly than now, on the roof of Notre Dame, with this girl's bright eyes on him. When, in the past, he had used aliases, they had been invented ones, springing new-minted from his resourceful mind. But this Duprez matter was different; Duprez was not an invented name.

Poe swallowed with a dry throat, hesitating.

"I shall be delighted to introduce you to Colonel Sauvagnac," Eleanor assured him.

A personal introduction from people of substance! For an impecunious soldier of fortune, it could make all the difference in the world. . . .

"Sir Bartle," said Eleanor gaily, "we'll take your friend there right now, shall we not?"

"No time like the present," said Sir Bartle, and took a

generous pinch of snuff to fortify himself against the descent of that hellish staircase.

"Come along, then, Mr. Duprez!" caroled Eleanor.

The logic of Necessity—

Poe drew in his breath, took up his greatcoat from the parapet. As he followed Eleanor and Sir Bartle, he looked out over the wide prospect of smoking chimney pots. He had an illusion that Paris was burning. But it was only his boats.

Seven

The butler who presently relieved Poe of his greatcoat and hat, in the vestibule of the fine old Faubourg Saint-Honoré mansion which was the headquarters of the Lafayette Circle, was an octogenarian, white-haired and stooped.

"A veteran," Colonel Sauvagnac told his callers, "of the Marquis's detachment at the fording of the Schuylkill."

"Oh, how marvelous!" said Eleanor.

Colonel Sauvagnac, a strong-looking man of Corsican appearance, immaculate in civilian attire, led the visitors into his salon, a lofty and handsome room with mullioned windows that looked out onto a shrubbery of frost-dusted laurels.

Above the wide fireplace, where logs glowed genially, the

flag of the United States and the tricolor of Revolutionary France hung from staves, and between them, in a place of honor on the paneled walls, was a framed parchment in copper-plate with illuminated capitals.

"The deed for the grant of American land," said Sauvagnac, "which Lafayette, on his last visit to America in his old age, received in person from the grateful hand of Mr. Jefferson."

The veteran of the Schuylkill returned, bearing a salver on which were a decanter and glasses. As the veteran withdrew, hobbling, Colonel Sauvagnac poured wine, while the three visitors looked around at the stands of weapons and the muskets, pistols, totem poles, feathered war bonnets, tomahawks and beaded medicine bags which graced the walls.

"Mementoes," said Sauvagnac, handing around the wine, "of the Marquis's adventures in North America. That large painting there depicts him when wounded in the leg at Brandy-wine Creek."

"Doesn't it just *thrill* you, Mr. Duprez?" Eleanor asked.

"Indeed, Miss Gerrard!" said Poe. "In*deed!*"

Moved, he emptied his glass at a gulp.

"That other large painting," said Colonel Sauvagnac, "—that shows the British general, Burgoyne, at the head of his Hessians and redcoats, surrendering his sword to General Gates at Saratoga."

"Hah!" snorted Sir Bartle. "Humph!"

"Oh, dear," said Eleanor, remorseful fingers to her lips, "how thoughtless we Americans are!"

"However," said Colonel Sauvagnac, "I'm happy to say, Sir Bartle, that General Gates returned General Burgoyne's sword to him."

"A gentlemanly act," said Sir Bartle, "for Burgoyne was betrayed from his rear—grossly let down by the dandies, rakes and tosspots of an imbecile Parliament sprawling in Whitehall!"

"Such is too often the fate of us soldiers," said Sauvagnac. "Here in France today we stagnate under the regime of Louis-Philippe, with his stockbroker's smug umbrella and his men-

tality of a provincial beadle. But, Mr. Duprez, sir—come, come
—your glass is empty!''

"May I remark, Colonel Sauvagnac," said Poe, permitting
his glass to be replenished, ''how beholden I am to Miss Gerrard
for this introduction—the more so since I aspire to the sympathy and influence of your distinguished Circle.''

"To what end, pray?'' asked Sauvagnac.

"To help me obtain a command—initially minor,'' Poe
conceded, ''—in the army of Poland, now beset by the Muscovite.''

Eleanor burst in excitedly, ''Colonel, Mr. Duprez is a graduate of West Point Military Academy!''

Sauvagnac looked at Poe with enhanced respect. ''A West
Point man, Mr. Duprez?''

And Poe, reckless now, threw down his gauntlet to destiny:
''I was well grounded there, sir, in the theory and practice of
warfare.''

"H'm,'' said Sauvagnac thoughtfully. ''Well, now, I'm
afraid I'm not personally acquainted with the Polish military
attaché here, Count Poniatowski—''

"Poniatowski?'' Drums rolled for Poe, cavalry trumpets
pealed ''Charge!'' in his ears, pennons flew and lances flashed
on a field of glory. ''Prince Poniatowski's Polish Lancers made
their name immortal at the storming of Somosierra!''

"You are learned in military history, Mr. Duprez,'' said
Sauvagnac, impressed.

"I *told* you!'' said Eleanor. Her eyes shone. ''West Point!''

"The count, I believe,'' said Sauvagnac, ''is of a cadet
branch of the great Poniatowski family. I regret, Mr. Duprez,
that I'm not in a position personally to further your aspirations.
However, I know a man who may be able to, and that's General
Aupick at the Invalides—our Minister of War. I could perhaps
arrange for you to meet him.''

Poe said, with fervor, ''It would place me eternally in your
debt, Colonel!''

"I'll see what I can do,'' said Sauvagnac. ''France is not

as yet directly involved in the Russo-Polish conflict, but I think General Aupick, in common with French public opinion, is opposed to Russian imperialism. When I inform him that a graduate of West Point seeks service in Poland, I think he'll at least receive you—unofficially, of course—probably at his home, number forty-four Rue Bourbon.''

Poe drained his glass.

At number forty-four Rue Bourbon, three nights later, a ball was in progress.

General Aupick, an erect, handsome man with a hawk nose and a cavalry moustache, the severity of his dark-blue uniform relieved only by epaulets, emerged from the great double doors which stood wide open to the ballroom where, under the chandeliers, dancers wove a glittering maze to the strains of violins.

In the foyer, a knee-breeched flunkey in livery was arranging with white-gloved hands an array of male cloaks and silk hats, walking-sticks, swords, helmets and shakos on a massive marquetry table.

"Jean," Aupick said sharply, "have you seen Madame Aupick?''

"Madame is in the withdrawing room, my General, with Monsieur Ancelle." Slightly hesitant, as one who bears dubious tidings, the flunkey added, "Monsieur Baudelaire has arrived.''

"Monsieur Charles?'' Aupick frowned, glanced at the sunburst wall clock, which showed a few minutes before nine, then crossed to a door, opened it and went into the spacious withdrawing room.

"Good evening, Charles,'' he said, closing the door behind him.

"Good evening, General,'¹ said Baudelaire.

His dark hair and youthful beard barbered to a nicety, he was standing—the picture of elegance, the mold of fashion, though not in evening dress—toying idly with his pink silk gloves.

Aupick gave the gloves a gimlet glance before turning to his wife, who, seated in a tapestried chair, was tapping her fan on her palm.

"Caroline," Aupick said, "this affair tonight is in the Polish cause. You should be with our guests."

A lovely woman who looked far younger than her husband, she smiled disarmingly. "I shall be coming in a moment, dear. Charles has arrived unexpectedly."

"So I see." Aupick took up a silver box from an occasional table, offered the box to Ancelle, the family lawyer, who, in evening black-and-white, had risen with a deferential smile at Aupick's entrance. "Cheroot, Ancelle?"

"Trichinopolies?" said Ancelle, a middle-aged man of unremarkable appearance, with sparse hair striping his head from a parting just above his left ear. "Why, thank you, General."

"You, Charles?" Aupick asked, proffering the box to his stepson.

"No, thank you," said Baudelaire.

"Poets' tastes," said Aupick, with irony, as he puffed his cheroot alight over the globed lamp on the claw-foot gilt table, "are more recondite, no doubt."

"Meaning peculiar?" said Baudelaire, with equal irony and a slight scornful smile.

Aupick said testily, "I did not say that. You put words into my mouth." He added, "Caroline, that clock on the mantel is two minutes slow."

"Oh, how remiss!" said Caroline, not perceptibly dismayed. "I must pay more attention to details."

"That would not be inappropriate," Aupick agreed drily, as he opened the clock glass. "I'm expecting a caller at nine—a Mr. Henry Lane Duprez. I shall receive him in my *bureau*."

"Please get rid of him as soon as possible," said Caroline. "This is not a night, dear, on which you should immerse yourself in business."

Aupick, correcting the laggard timepiece with a firm forefinger, said, "You know, Charles, I have no quarrel with versifying in its patriotic aspects. The heroic ode no doubt serves some purpose." Closing the clock glass, he turned to his stepson. "On the other hand, I question whether the composition of triolets and roundelays is a worthy occupation for a virile man."

The word virile touched Baudelaire on a private sore spot, and he replied tartly, "So you've remarked before, General—to the point of tedium."

"Charles!" murmured Caroline, with a glance of reproach at her son.

Aupick's face darkened. And Ancelle said, hastily sycophant, "The Muses make alluring mistresses, Monsieur Charles, but flighty helpmeets."

"I admit," said Aupick, occupying a commanding position on the hearthrug, his back to the fire, "that I've had scant leisure to disport myself with the Muses. My time has been claimed by weightier issues."

"And what issues!" anthemed Ancelle. "From cadet to general—and perhaps soon, I've heard whispered, Ambassador to Madrid or Constantinople!"

"Ancelle," Aupick said, frowning, "you should know better, as a legal man, than to repeat the tittle-tattle of diplomatic anterooms."

"General, I beg you"—Ancelle groveled a little—"overlook my unhappy indiscretion!"

"Is this true, dear?" Caroline asked her husband.

"There's talk," he said, "of giving me Madrid or the Sublime Porte, one or the other." He shrugged carelessly, but puffed at his cheroot with a certain complacence before resuming his admonition to his stepson. "However, as I was about to remark, it seems to me that what passes for the Arts in Paris nowadays wallows wilfully in the sewer. Frankly, Charles, your own choice of subjects—"

"With respect, General," said Baudelaire, without respect, "what do *you* know of my subjects? I haven't yet published."

Caroline blushed guiltily. "Charles, your step-papa has seen one or two of your manuscripts."

Baudelaire's fine dark eyes shot her a look of fury.

"They disquiet me," said Aupick. "They mock religion, deride civil order, laud indulgence in sexual license and the stupefying drugs—"

"Decadence!" said Ancelle, shaking his head. "Decadence!"

"At all events, Charles," said Aupick, "I doubt if exalted art is best sought by lounging in cafés with lewd companions all day and lolling in the embrace of harlots half the night."

"Why half?" said Baudelaire. "I thought you put a premium on virility, General."

"*Black* harlots, moreover," said Aupick, with a scowl.

"Black?" said Caroline, fanning herself rapidly. "Charles, what is this I hear?"

Baudelaire, ignoring the question, said with lofty contempt, "I must congratulate the General on the efficiency of his spies."

Aupick drew himself yet more erect, bristling, but just then, perhaps fortunately, the clock began to chime—and simultaneously, through the mellow chiming and the faint sound of music from the ballroom, a bell jangled silvery in the foyer.

"That," Aupick said, "will be my caller. Caroline, while I deal with him, you will oblige me by attending upon our guests."

His hand on the glass doorknob, he turned to look at Baudelaire, who had turned his back and was examining the volumes in the bookcase.

"It will be refreshing," said Aupick cuttingly, "to talk with this American gentleman—an ardent and ambitious officer out of West Point!"

He opened the door, slammed it behind him, glanced through the wide doorway to the ballroom, where the dancers, weaving their supple convolutions, rose upon tiptoe and sank in genuflections.

Aupick's stern gaze moved to his caller, who was being relieved of his caped greatcoat and conspicuously transatlantic hat by Jean, the flunkey. Against the glitter of uniforms in the ball-room, the shimmer of silken gowns and the sheen of satin, the wink of gems on bosoms creamily undulant under the chandeliers, Poe in his unrelieved black, with his cadaverous pallor and his portentous brow, had a certain ominous distinction.

Aupick moved forward. "Mr. Henry Lane Duprez, I presume."

"General Aupick," said Poe, and clicked his heels, with a stiff military bow.

Aupick motioned to a door across the hall. "We'll talk in my *bureau.*"

"Commanded," said Poe crisply.

He followed Aupick.

Caroline, in the withdrawing room, was reproaching her son.

"Oh, Charles, why must you always provoke the general?"

"On the off chance," said Baudelaire, "that he'll have a stroke—preferably fatal."

"Charles, you go too far!"

"The artist can never go too far. That is his merit." Baudelaire's irritation broke through his affected suavity. "What the devil d'you mean, Mother, by showing your ineffable husband my manuscripts?"

"Darling, I didn't! They were among the few things you left here, and he chanced upon them."

"You mean he quested for them—poked and pried for them, sniffed like a truffle hound in the nooks and crannies in the hope of finding something of mine with which to scandalize himself!"

Caroline sighed hopelessly. "Oh, Charles, if only you would understand! He's really fond of you, concerned about you—"

"So he makes me a derision to my friends," said Baudelaire bitterly, "by trapping me into this squalid arrangement about the money my father left me!"

"Ah, poor François!" Caroline fanned away the memory of

her first husband, knowing that that worthy man would have started up out of his grave if he knew what was happening to the pile he had accumulated in the course of an industrious but tiresome lifetime. "Charles," she said, "you came into your capital at twenty-one—"

"I matured early," said Baudelaire.

"I sometimes wonder!" said Caroline. "In a little over three years you've squandered nearly half of your fortune. And, even so, you have debts!"

"Debts are in fashion."

"But, Charles, consider—you *agreed* to the trust whereby Monsieur Ancelle here now administers what remains of your capital."

"A prudent step," said Ancelle, with a wise look, "and taken none too soon!"

"Oh, for God's sake," said Baudelaire. "The arrangement was forced on me by the general. I didn't realize its implications. The indignity of it! The mere impracticality! My apartment is in the heart of Paris—in the Ile Saint-Louis. Yet now, every time I need money, I'm required to present myself in person to Monsieur Ancelle—tot up budgets—furnish him with the chapter and verse of my expenses—"

"Oh, come now," protested Ancelle, "come, come, Monsieur Charles!"

"And his legal lair is in Neuilly," said Baudelaire. "Neuilly! On the dismal outskirts of Paris, compelling me to hire cabs and then hector with him to get sous for the fare!"

"Oh, Charles," said Caroline, "you do so exaggerate!"

"Exaggerate? I assure you, my respected mater, it's impossible to exaggerate the humiliation I feel in the presence of my friends. Roger de Beauvoir, for example—"

"Young Roger de Beauvoir," sighed Caroline, "inherited a great fortune, whereas your own patrimony, my dear boy, was at best modest—"

"And is rendered now, by the follies of youth," said Ancelle, with glum relish, "meager!"

"This house! *Parbleu,* this house!" Distracted, Baudelaire strode the floor, waving his gloves about. "What sympathy do I find—what understanding—what even elementary kindness? I come here, my work harassed by duns, my pockets empty—hard put to it for a crust to keep body and soul together—"

"Oh, Charles!" Caroline could not help laughing. She offered him, mischievously, a comfit box from the table. "Have a *marron glacé!*"

Baudelaire checked, deeply offended.

"Try, Mother," he said; "make at least some *slight* effort to control your frivolity and treat serious matters seriously!"

But she could not stop laughing behind her fan.

Baudelaire, incensed, dashed his gloves to the floor.

Ancelle, looking askance at mother and son, tiptoed tactfully from the room.

In his *bureau,* General Aupick, sitting at his desk under a portrait of the bourgeois monarch Louis-Philippe in a silk hat, with a furled umbrella, looked searchingly at his caller seated on the other side of the desk.

Plans of redoubts, saps and casemates covered the walls.

Aupick frowned. He tapped ash from his cheroot into the sawn half of a bomb casing on his desk, and said slowly, "Am I to understand, then, Mr. Duprez, that you were *not* in fact graduated from West Point with a commission in the United States Army?"

"The position," said Poe, prevaricating, "is somewhat unusual. I—"

"Come, sir," said Aupick, "either you held a commission or you did not."

"Unfortunately," said Poe, "though I was far advanced in the curriculum, circumstances conspired to compel my withdrawal. The commandant was considerably agitated."

"Did he express his concern in writing?"

"As a military man, sir," Poe said, with the feeling of

fighting a desperate rear-guard action, "he was averse to paper-work."

"Then the fact is, Mr. Duprez, you càn show me no documentary evidence whatever of your West Point cadetship?"

"General Aupick," Poe said coldly, "you have my word for it."

Aupick, thoughtful, rearranged the models of the siege train —cannons, mortars, ambulance, field kitchens, commissary carts and funeral wagon—which toiled across the red leather field of his desktop.

"Mr. Duprez," he said heavily, "please understand my position. The Polish military attaché, Count Leopold Poniatowski, is a personal friend of mine—"

"Then I beseech you, General," said Poe, with fervor, "put in a good word for me! Surely, sir, that's little enough to ask?"

"I have a duty to the count," said Aupick. "Europe is full of military adventurers—booty-seeking mercenaries, mere jackals of Mars—"

"Jackal?" Poe reared, insulted. "I'm no jackal! *Booty,* sir? I can imagine nothing of less consequence!"

In his excitement, he was seized by coughing. Shaken by the paroxysm, he sank back in his chair, his handkerchief to his moustache.

Aupick said grimly, "That's a graveyard cough you have there."

"Yet you question my right," gasped Poe, hoarse and furious, "to die with my boots on!"

In the withdrawing room, where they were alone together, mother and son had sailed into calmer waters, and Caroline was saying, "Now, tell me honestly, Charles—are you really without funds?"

"Can you imagine anything else," said Baudelaire, "that would have brought me back to this house?"

Her pretty eyes looked wistfully over her fan at her handsome son. "Don't *I* mean anything to you, Charles?"

"You are a captive beauty in an ogre's cave," Baudelaire assured her, "but I enjoy you most when you elude the ogre and come to visit me in my apartment."

"The general says it's a den of licentious indulgences," said Caroline. "He forbids me to go there."

"Then come by night," suggested Baudelaire, "hooded and masked—a mysterious charmer to captivate my 'lewd companions'!"

"The general *is* unreasonable," Caroline admitted. "After all, I'm your mother."

Baudelaire took her fan from her and kissed her palm.

"I love the feel of your little beard," said Caroline. "It's so silky."

"And I love mothers," said Baudelaire. "They're so unselfish."

"Stop hinting! Oh, Charles, I'm worried about you!"

"Fifty louis," said Baudelaire, "and your worries are over."

"A mother shouldn't pay her son's debts," said Caroline severely.

"What the world says one shouldn't do," Baudelaire said, "one should do on principle."

"Charles, you're incorrigible!"

"*You* brought me up." With a care for the crease in his trousers, he dropped gracefully on one knee before her, kissed her, smiled into her eyes. "Fifty louis, Mama?"

"You're awful!" She smoothed back the lock of hair slanting across his brow, opened a drawer of the occasional table, took out a gold-net purse. "Your women will ruin you, Charles."

"You're my woman—the woman who made me."

She giggled. "François had a hand in it."

"A what?"

"Charles, *really!*" said Caroline, a little shocked.

Baudelaire reached for the purse, but she held it behind her. "No! Tell me, first—what's this about a black girl?"

"Such a question is unbecoming from a mother."

"So there *is* a black girl! Who is she, Charles?"

"This interrogation must cease," said Baudelaire. "The purse, Mama!"

"But, Charles—why black?"

"The general, in his wisdom," said Baudelaire, "dispatched me on a voyage to India—to make my fortune in the trade with the nabobs of Pondicherry."

"Poor man, he wanted to get you away from the Roger de Beauvoir set. What a hope! You only went as far as Mauritius."

"The captain and I were incompatible." Baudelaire sighed, unsmiling now. "Yes, I left the ship at Mauritius—"

"Did something happen there, to bring you back?" Troubled, she cupped his beard in her hand, raising his chin. "I wonder sometimes, darling, is anything the matter?"

"Yes." He kissed her palm. "I need fifty louis."

"To spend on your black girl?" she said jealously.

"The voyage," said Baudelaire, "broadened my mind."

As though become now aware of the strains of a waltz floating faintly from the ballroom, he rose suddenly, pulled Caroline up roughly from the chair, and whirled her about the room in a wild dance, his cheek to hers, his right hand groping for the purse which she held tauntingly behind her back.

Abruptly, the music swelled loud.

They checked involuntarily, looking toward the door, Caroline breathless, her hair a little disheveled.

The door was open. General Aupick stood there, a thundercloud with epaulets.

Eight

"Charles! Take your hands off my wife," Aupick said grimly. "This instant!"

Dismayed, Caroline pushed Baudelaire back from her, but not before he had possessed himself of the purse.

"By God!" said Aupick, advancing into the room. "I'll shoot any man, stepson or no, I see dancing with my wife like that!"

"A one-man firing squad," said Baudelaire.

From the doorway Ancelle peeped in, agog for intimations of incest in the withdrawing room.

"If you want to dance," Aupick said harshly, "dress appropriately, Charles—and do it in the ballroom."

"Your suggestion would be more amusing, General," said

Baudelaire, "if it referred to *un*dressing in the ballroom—as a communal exercise to the music of a mazurka. Don't you think so, Mama?"

But Caroline's eyes were on her angry husband.

Baudelaire smiled. Toying with the gold-net purse, he kissed her lightly on the lips.

"Oh, Charles!" she said, and moved away to a pier glass, gilt-framed on the wall.

"That purse," said Aupick. "Give it to me, Charles."

"Should I, Mama?" Baudelaire asked, tossing up the purse and catching it. "Is the general overdrawn? Or merely overwrought?"

Caroline, repairing her coiffure before the pier glass, looked at the reflections of her husband and son in confrontation and murmured, with lips pursed about a hairpin, "They both so *exaggerate* everything!"

"Charles!" rasped Aupick. "That purse! You may be able to get around your mother, but you can't get around me!"

Circling around him warily, Baudelaire said, "Mama, come and visit me in more aesthetic surroundings."

"You'll do no such thing, Caroline," Aupick commanded, as he pivoted, hard eyes on Baudelaire and an adamant hand extended for the purse. "You'll keep away from his kennel of posturing lapdogs!"

"Come soon, Mama," said Baudelaire—and, having got successfully around Aupick to the doorway, walked out past Ancelle.

The lawyer shrank back from him, for fear of guilt by association. In the ballroom the violins lilted, the piccolos piped, the dancers twirled, all heedless of a family's disgraces. Avid for more of them, Ancelle craned for another look into the withdrawing room—only to be pushed rudely out of the way by Aupick, emerging.

"Charles!"

Baudelaire, in the foyer, was taking up his purple-lined cloak, his silk hat and his ebony stick from the marquetry table.

Nearby, Poe was being helped on with his caped greatcoat by Jean, the flunkey.

"Charles," Aupick said, with iron self-control, "come back in here!"

Poe, taking his lofty hat from the flunkey, looked with cavernous eyes at Aupick, then at Baudelaire, who slung his cloak over his arm and walked to the street door. Opening it, Baudelaire turned.

"Have no fear, General," he said. "Posterity will have to reckon with me."

He put on his silk hat at a jaunty angle and, with a valedictory flourish of his pink silk gloves retrieved from the carpet of the withdrawing room, walked down the steps, leaving the door wide open, and turned to the right into the darkness of the Rue Bourbon.

Poe, who was taut with rage on his own account, took the opportunity to make his personal position clear.

"General Aupick," he said icily, "you have seen fit to impugn my veracity and denigrate my health—"

A tall, blond man in lancer's scarlet uniform, emerging at that moment from the ballroom, checked sharply.

"I shall not," said Poe, with a dire look, "enter this house again!"

He clapped on his hat and, turning to the open door, stalked down the steps and turned to the right into the darkness of the Rue Bourbon.

The blond lancer screwed a single eyeglass into his eye.

"General Aupick," he said, "should you be in need of a friend in any small forthcoming affair—"

"Bah!" said Aupick. "An American—some grotesque Yankee—a flimsy adventurer with an auctioned sword! Thank you, but we shall hear no more of that fellow, my dear Poniatowski."

On the other hand, Baudelaire, walking along the Rue Bourbon toward the wan glimmer of a wall-bracket gas lanthorn, became aware of footfalls behind him. They kept pace with his own. He frowned.

Reaching the cone of wan luminance cast by the lamp on this misty, chill night, he paused, listening. The footfalls came on, ringing louder in the silent street.

Baudelaire whirled around, presenting his stick at Poe's breastbone as he stalked gauntly into the dim illumination.

"Halt! You are following me!"

"Following you? You flatter yourself, sir!"

"You were closeted with General Aupick!'

"What business is that of yours?"

"You know very well what business, Monsieur Henri Lane Duprez," sneered Baudelaire, "'ardent and ambitious soldier.' !"

"I warn you," Poe said dangerously. "Stop pointing that stick at me. My patience is limited."

"*Your* patience? By God, when my stepfather sets his boot-licking bravos to sneaking around after me—"

"Bravos?"

"Spies!"

"Enough! I'll have that stick!"

Poe grabbed for it. Baudelaire held it tighter. Shuffling and wrestling, they executed a war dance under the street lamp as they contended for possession of the stick, which, with a sudden *whoosh,* parted in two. Off balance, they staggered back from each other, Poe in possession of the sheath, Baudelaire of the rapier.

It caught the light with a steely sparkle.

"Now spy," said Baudelaire, "I'll split your gizzard like a turkey's!"

"Cook's work," said Poe. "Lay on, scullion—fit stepson for a boorish butcher!"

"Boorish?" Sensing cross-purposes here, Baudelaire withheld the *coup de grâce.* "You refer to Aupick?"

"A blot on his regiment," panted Poe, breathless from conflict. "I've been given the lie under his smug roof!"

"That roof," said Baudelaire, "shelters my mother."

"Then God help the lady!"

"Amen to that," agreed Baudelaire. "Sir, it seems I've misunderstood you."

"So many do," gasped Poe, and let fall the stick sheath to fumble for his handkerchief as his cough overcame him.

Baudelaire picked up the sheath, restored his gold-knobbed rapier to it and looked at Poe, who was strangling into his handkerchief.

"Mr. Duprez," Baudelaire said, as Poe's paroxysm subsided, "what is the American attitude to alcohol?"

"We give thanks for it," Poe wheezed, wiping his eyes and moustache, "to God from Whom all blessings flow."

"Shall we, then," suggested Baudelaire, "seek 'lewd companionship' at the Café Momus and drink damnation to Aupick? I happen to be in funds."

Poe pocketed his handkerchief with alacrity. "Sir, I happen to be in the mood."

They appraised each other for a moment in the glimmer from the lamp. They smiled. Then, unaware that their meeting had brought together literature's most ingenious plot-maker and a young poet sorely in need of a plot to liberate his inheritance, they walked off together into the night.

Next day was a Sunday.

Far off in Naples, a girl whom Poe might have recognized from a certain miniature illicitly in his possession, though he had forgotten her name, was among those members of a church congregation who lingered on the steps after the service.

With its peeling, pinkish façade, its open belfry of verdigrised bells, the church was one favored by the English winter colony, and the temperate sunshine of February in these climes beamed on top hats and the jet beads of Sabbath bonnets. When gentlefolk meet, compliments are exchanged, and the small groups on the church steps gossiped with the ease which is the divine right of those who have made their peace with things spiritual and a reasonable contribution to the offertory plate.

Over the cone of Vesuvius loitered a curl of smoke. To Kate Casteign, who alone of those present seemed troubled in her mind, the smoke looked like a question mark pendent in the blue. Questioning what, she wondered—the efficacy of holy water to quench smoldering fires in a bereft bosom?

She put a hand to the bosom, and, inattentive to the chatter of her companions—the pretty sisters, Elena and Anunciata, and their dashing brother Tonio, of the princely Pascarella family—her gray eyes wandered to the old Castello looming on its bluff above a huddle of roofs that fell away steeply to where ships clustered in the curve of the mole. The sea stretched beyond, with a shifting and languid sparkle, to where Capri lifted its cliffs in the middle distance.

"Kate," said Elena, "we must go. Our *carrozza* is waiting."

Roused from her muse, Kate exchanged kisses with the Pascarella girls, her hair seeming the fairer for contrast with their brunette beauty and black lace head-veils.

Tonio, an ardent glow in his brown eyes as he bowed over Kate's hand, said, "You'll remind your mother, will you not, that we expect you at one o'clock for luncheon?"

"Of course, Tonio," Kate said, and stood watching as he joined his sisters in the open carriage and it jingled away.

Behind her, and farther up the church steps, her mother, Lady Casteign, was talking to the British consul, Mr. Albany Bryce, who took a letter from his pocket. He gave the letter to Lady Casteign, who flipped up the lenses of her lorgnette to scrutinize the address, then placed the missive in her reticule.

Leaving Mr. Bryce holding his hat uplifted, she descended the steps to join her daughter.

"Kate, we'll take the air in the public gardens. It will give us an appetite."

In the gardens, the voices of children at play, scampering in their Sunday-best frocks and sailor suits, mingled with the cries of tattered youths, bronzed and beautiful, offering joyrides in little Neapolitan carts intricately painted and drawn by morose donkeys such as the one that had carried Jesus into Jerusalem.

"We will sit down on a seat," said Lady Casteign, as she sauntered with Kate in the sunshine and the speckled shade of date palms. "I have something for you."

She paused at a marble seat but, on noting the vigorous male endowments of the marble Discobolus who impended over it, she chose another seat a little farther on, for there was no point in putting ideas into the head of an unmarried daughter already quite difficult enough.

"Something for me?" asked Kate, as they sat down.

"Mr. Albany Bryce," said Lady Casteign, opening her reticule, "gave me this letter, addressed in care of the Consulate. It is franked 'Paris.' "

"For me?" Kate snatched the letter. "At last!" But as she looked at the address, her excitement ebbed. "Oh! It's not from—"

"It's not addressed in the handwriting of Henry Lane Duprez," said Lady Casteign, "if that's what you mean."

"Excuse me," said Kate—and, breaking the red blob of the seal, unfolded the letter.

Lady Casteign inspected the passing throng through her lorgnette and the half veil which bisected her commanding nose.

"I'm rather glad," she remarked, "that we decided to winter in Italy rather than Spain. Not that there's much to choose between them, but at least, thank heavens, they're not America."

"I *like* America and Americans," said Kate, reading her letter, "and you shouldn't say unamiable things about their country."

"Which 'tis of them," said Lady Casteign. "Who is your letter from?"

"Eleanor Gerrard. She's in Paris."

"Chaperoned, I trust?"

"She seems to be with somebody called Sir Bartle Mole."

"A male chaperon?"

"I expect he does the best he can," said Kate absently.

"As much as she'll allow him to, no doubt," said Lady Casteign, with a sniff.

"Oh, Mother, listen—listen to this!" Kate read aloud from her letter: " 'And there—on the roof of Notre Dame, of all places—Sir Bartle and I met an interesting American who's just dying to wield his sword on the battlefields of Poland. When we came upon him, he was doing a kind of dance—' "

"A sword dance, one assumes," said Lady Casteign.

"Please listen," begged Kate, and read on: " '—though something tense and haunted in the look of his eyes gave me a feeling that he's trying to escape from the world of dear, familiar things and just bury himself—' "

"The Russians will take care of burial for him," said Lady Casteign, "if he goes meddling in their battles."

" 'He's a Mr. Henry Lane Duprez,' " Kate read out, with emphasis, from the letter, " 'of New Orleans!' " She looked at her mother.

"Henry Duprez?" said Lady Casteign. "How excessively odd!"

"Isn't it?" said Kate. She had grown pale. "Tell me, Mother, why did Mr. Bryce give this letter to *you* when it's addressed to *me*?"

"You were chattering to the Pascarellas."

"Would you have given me this letter if it'd been addressed in Henry's handwriting?"

"Kate! How dare you!"

"Mother," Kate said levelly, "that's not an answer."

"My child," said Lady Casteign, "I could by no means, as the widow of a distinguished British diplomatist, condone Henry Duprez's involvement with his—his concubine on the plantation, flaunting her impudent smile and her all too vivid head bandanna!"

"Oh, Mother, we've been over and over all that! If only—"

"I brought you back to Europe in the hope that you would form some less disagreeable attachment."

"I blame myself—for running away."

"Running away, nonsense! You have your pride, I hope!"

"My pride was what was hurt," said Kate, "but when I think of Henry, I seem to grow less proud every day."

"Kate, the philanderer Duprez blinds you to finer opportunities. Tonio Pascarella, the most eligible youth in Naples, grows bright-eyed every time he sees you."

"He grows bright-eyed at every woman. It's because he's Italian. It's the way they are," said Kate. "Mother, can't you grasp the fact that there's only one man I *love?*"

"Hopeless," said Lady Casteign. "Kate, it is utterly hopeless, as I've come to realize during these past few months." She sighed. "Oh, well, I suppose I may as well resign myself to the situation and accept the inevitable."

She opened her reticule, took out a sheaf of letters.

Kate snatched them. "I *knew* it! You've been intercepting them! I felt *sure* Henry would write!"

"God send," said Lady Casteign, "that I'm not making a dreadful mistake in this moment."

"Just look!" said Kate. "All these! Unopened! Unanswered! Mother, how *could* you?"

"So long," said Lady Casteign, "as I thought there was a chance of your finding a husband not vested with the *droit du seigneur* available to the heir of a tobacco plantation swarming with indentured doxies in a warm, morally debilitating climate—"

"Poor Henry!" said Kate. "No wonder he feels tense and haunted, because I've felt just the same! If *I* were a man and had lost me, *I'd* want to die in battle, and forget it all, and bury myself—just like Henry! He must be stopped! I simply will *not* allow him to throw his life away because he's lost me, because he *hasn't!* Mother, whatever you say, I will leave for Paris this instant!"

"You will do nothing," said Lady Casteign, "so disobliging to the Pascarellas. We are bespoke to them for luncheon."

"I've been weak, Mother," said Kate, "but now the time's come when I must take a firm line."

"The line you take," said Lady Casteign, "will be directly to the Pascarello *palazzo*. It's getting on for luncheon time." She rose. "Tomorrow we'll see about getting berths in the ship which sails regularly from Naples here to Nice, where we can connect with the Paris mail coach."

"Mother!" Kate's eyes sparkled. "You mean it?"

"I can no longer endure the present situation," said Lady Casteign. "It must be brought to a head. Henry Duprez must be broken to harness or else permanently disposed of, as the case may be."

"Ah, che bella ragazza!" called a beautiful youth, passing by, tousle-headed and barefoot, leading his donkey cart.

He tossed Kate a flower he had been holding between the faultless teeth he now displayed to her in a seductive smile.

"Bellissima!" he called, reeling a little, to show he was overcome.

"Kate," said Lady Casteign haughtily, "ignore that pert fellow!"

"Yes, Mother," said Kate, as they walked away together among the sunlit date palms and marble-white statues. "But did you notice how his eyes shone? That's what I meant about Italians."

Nine

"Les journaux!" piped the gamine newspaper-seller over the din of voices and laughter in the Café Momus. *"Tous les journaux! Ici les journaux de Paris!"*

In the Rue des Prêtres, outside the steamy windows, a cold rain was falling, but the café was snug with the warmth from two large stoves and the clay pipes fashionable among the bohemians.

Prodigal of hair and beard, their velvet berets variously tilted, their corduroy jackets out at the elbows, the habitués, mostly youthful, argued with fervor over the marble-topped tables, to the admiration of the clinging girls who were their adoring models and mistresses, faithful unto Tuesday next, in the high adventure of Art.

"L'Artiste," shrilled the gamine, circulating among the tables, satchel over her shoulder, papers under her arm. *"L'Esprit Public—Le Bulletin des Arts—Corsaire-Satan—"*

At a table by the window, Baudelaire, despite the silk hat on the back of his head and the gold-knobbed stick and pink silk gloves of a dedicated dandy, seemed nevertheless at ease among the shoestring fellowship of the pen, the brush, and the sculptors of colossal nudes.

But Poe, the senior of the others at this table by ten years or so, cut a noticeably alien figure among them, partly because of the sobriety of his garb. His beaver hat stood towering among the glasses on the table, and a large lobster was perched on the crown of the hat. The lobster, which wore a bow and was attached to a ribbon held by an epicene individual of an age rendered uncertain by subtle depravities, also seemed a little out of its element. It appeared to recognize in Poe a like displacement, for its stalked eyeballs regarded him steadily, and occasionally it saluted him with a languid antenna.

"Why a lobster?" said O'Neddy. An erotic novelist as yet unpublished, either under his own name, Théophile Dondey, or the fractured anagram of it which he used as a pseudonym on his disturbing works, he blinked through glasses that magnified his eyes at the lobster's master. "Crespigny, you carry nonconformism almost to the point of affectation. Lobsters aren't pets."

"Cats make me sneeze, and dogs bark," Crespigny explained, in his ingratiating falsetto. "I have, like most composers, exceptionally sensitive ears." He adjusted the crustacean's bow affectionately. "Haven't I, my little Critic?"

"Critic?" said Théodore de Banville. "Is that his name?"

"Except when he makes scraping noises in his little box when I'm counting crochets in an aria for my divine opera," said Armand Crespigny. "Then I'm vexed at him, and I spit upon him and call him Crétin!"

The lobster's eyes jerked from side to side on their stalks.

"You've hurt his feelings," said Jules Champfleury. "He'll

shed salt tears. Tell me, Armand—how did you ascertain his gender?"

"Don't be rude, Jules," simpered Crespigny, "you naughty boy!"

"Bizarre," said Poe.

"The beautiful, Henri," Baudelaire retorted, "is always bizarre."

"But the bizarre, Charles," said Poe, "is not always beautiful."

"Baudelaire's American is saying spiteful things about you," Crespigny told his pet. "I shan't let you sit on his hat. I shall take you away, before he boils and eats you."

"With mayonnaise," said Baudelaire, as the composer minced off to introduce his pet at more sympathetic tables. "A Lucullan banquet!"

Poe retrieved his hat and set it, for safety, squarely on his great brow—as the gamine came to the table, piping, "*Les journaux! Le Moniteur—Corsaire-Satin—*"

O'Neddy, Banville and Champfleury seized papers from her and, with the breathless suspense engendered by the submission of unsolicited manuscripts, searched eagerly through the pages.

"Simone, my love," said Baudelaire, taking her hand, pressing coins into it, and closing her bitten fingernails over them tenderly. "My precious gamine with the stars of Paris in your eyes!"

"*Merde!*" said the starry-eyed Simone.

"And its argot," said Baudelaire, as the gamine moved off, "so enchantingly pithy on her rosebud lips!" He looked at the trio searching through the newspapers and said to Poe, "Henri, regard these tyros—actually hoping to find their 'prentice works immortalized by printer's devils!"

Poe smiled wryly. How often had he known the same feeling —in the Philadelphia from which he had departed with every intention of applying for a sub-editorship on the *New York Daily*

Mirror, edited by Nathaniel Parker Willis. How inconceivably remote all that now seemed!

O'Neddy crumpled his paper angrily. "Editors! Purblind imbeciles!"

"That from O'Neddy," said Baudelaire tolerantly. "D'you know, Henri, he goes to bed with those owlish glasses on."

"My dreams are in color," claimed the youthful O'Neddy. "I should hate to miss seeing them."

Banville cast his paper aside with disgust. "Editors would like to see all writers with aspirations to style boiled in their own ink!"

"Profit by my example, *mes amis,*" Baudelaire comforted them. "Don't rush into print. Our early works return, like our illegitimate children, to mortify us in our maturity."

"All very well for you, Baudelaire," said Banville. "You came into money."

"And we haven't seen much of you in the *quartier,*" added Champfleury, "ever since."

Baudelaire looked pained—but, before he could reply, Banville jumped up from his chair.

"On your feet, triflers," he said. "Here comes Eugène Sue! A bow, please, for the Golden Quill—the Idol of the Popular Press!"

Sue, a bearded man in his early forties, with a look about him of character, distinction and success, came to the table—to florid obeisances from Baudelaire, Banville, Champfleury and O'Neddy, while Poe, somewhat at a loss, stood holding his hat aloft.

"At ease, aspirants," said Sue goodhumoredly. "What, are those absinthe glasses I see on the table? Take heed to your livers!"

"Such piety!" said Banville. "As if you hadn't been in your time the most notorious dandy and sponge in Paris!"

"I discovered my limitations," said Sue, "in time to salvage my partially ruined intellect."

"Eugène," said Baudelaire, "meet my American, Henri Lane Duprez, the favorite son of New Orleans. He's been my cherished guest for the past week or two, and I hope will remain so. He's a military man."

"Temporarily out of employment, Monsieur Sue," Poe confessed.

"Your sword won't rust for long, Monsieur Duprez," said Sue. "Our monarch totters on his cashbox throne. Revolution smolders in the alleys. I smell it."

"To the barricades!" enthused Champfleury, Banville and O'Neddy.

"Death to General Aupick!" said Baudelaire—and meant it.

Banville said to Poe, "As a military man, Duprez, you behold a fellow warrior in Eugène Sue. He's seen action—in the War of Greek Independence."

"As a naval surgeon, Monsieur Duprez," Sue said, "a mere sawbones—at Navarino, under Rear-Admiral Count de Rigny."

"The experience whetted Sue's taste for sensation," said Baudelaire, "which he now pours into his newspaper serial, *The Rival Races.*"

"That *feuilleton* is the talk of the town," said O'Neddy, blinking enviously at Sue through his glasses, "—the history of the Franks and the Gauls, bloodily fictionalized."

"The longest serial since Josephus was caught short of pogroms," said Champfleury. "All Gaul is divided into three parts, but Sue's had the gall to spin it out to a hundred and forty!"

"And I'm just beginning to get into it," said Sue. "Thank God for the daily press, for I have an expensive mistress to support."

"*The Rival Races,*" said Poe, his imagination warmed, "—a mighty tantalizing title, Monsieur Sue!"

Baudelaire, delighted, clapped a pink-gloved hand possessively on Poe's shoulder. "There! You see, you fellows, why my

American enchants me? He has an instinctive response to literature, quite amazing in a professional soldier.''

"Herodotus wrote and Thucydides was a penny-a-liner,"
said Sue. "Soldiers both! Come, gentlemen—I'll buy a drink."

"Eugène, it desolates me," said Baudelaire, to Poe's
regret, "but I must needs venture out intrepidly to the blasted
heaths of Neuilly and beard a legal person who lurks there in
the odor of usury. I must take my American with me for moral
support in a slight domestic crisis. Come, Henri—once more unto
the breach in the purse strings, dear friend! *Au revoir, tout le
monde!*"

"*Au revoir! Au revoir, Duprez!*" chorused the literati. "*Au
revoir, Baudelaire! A bientôt, hein?*"

Poe and Baudelaire went out together into the rain.

"An odd contrast, those two," said Banville, watching
through the steamy window as Poe and Baudelaire walked away
over the puddled *pavé* of the Rue des Prêtres. "So it seems the
rumor's true, then—Baudelaire's patrimony is now administered
by the Aupick family lawyer."

"What's left of it," said Champfleury. "The lawyer, I believe, keeps a tight clutch on the residue. Why else would Baudelaire forsake the expensive circle of Roger de Beauvoir and his
gilded ilk, and reappear here at the Momus?"

"Does his peculiar American have money?" asked Banville.

"Not a sou to his name," said Champfleury; "nothing but a
blade for hire, and no takers. I hear he applied to General Aupick
for martial employment and was kicked out of the house."

"And Baudelaire took him in?" said Banville. "I'd have
thought he had quite enough calls on his purse in his present
circumstances—with his black lady to support and that out-
rageously luxurious apartment of his."

"Two apartments," said O'Neddy, "his own in the Ile
Saint-Louis, and the little love nest he furnished exotically in
the Place Dauphine."

"For his black beauty," said Champfleury, "—to have her nice and handy." He laughed. "His delicious mama would be green-eyed if she knew about Jeanne Duval."

"I saw her in the ballet at the Théâtre du Panthéon," said O'Neddy. "Baudelaire keeps her very dark."

"*Le mot juste!*" said Banville.

"I don't blame him," said O'Neddy. "She has an exotic charm."

"And makes any man free of it," said Champfleury, "who happens to take her fancy."

"Which, rumor hath it, is currently," said Banville, "a certain gorilla." He shrugged. "It appeals, no doubt, to her generous tropical nature."

"Baudelaire must be crazy," said O'Neddy, blinking through his glasses "Why does he put up with her notorious infidelities?"

"I could venture a guess," said Champfleury. "I've heard whispers about Charles Baudelaire since he made that mysterious voyage to wherever it was."

"He was forced into that by General Aupick," said O'Neddy, "to get him away from the Roger de Beauvoir set and . . . make a man of him."

"That's what's so ironic," said Champfleury, with a grin. "Nothing's so unmanning as the stealthy wounds of Venus!"

Eugène Sue slapped his hand down suddenly on the table.

"*That* will do," he said. "Good God, you stripling men of letters tattle like a coven of old witches picking rags under the arches of the Pont-Neuf! Desist—and I'll buy you beer."

"I'd prefer absinthe," said Banville.

"Poison," said Sue. "As an ex-medical man, and a reformed character in my judicious middle age, I prescribe the wholesome hop."

"Killjoy," said Banville.

"You know," said O'Neddy, his myopic, slightly protuberant eyes thoughtful as he polished his glasses, "Baudelaire lives dangerously."

"Charles Baudelaire," Sue said, "has talent. And *that* is his danger. *Garçon!*"

Baudelaire and his American, returning later that same day from an acrimonious interview with Monsieur Ancelle at Neuilly, were walking across the old gray stone bridge to the Ile Saint-Louis, where Baudelaire had his apartment in the ancient and gracious precincts of the Hôtel Lauzun.

They had left Ancelle, who had yielded under moral pressure, contemplating his somewhat depleted coffers; and over a well-irrigated lunch at a favorite haunt of Baudelaire's in the Bas Breau they had celebrated the lawyer's chagrin.

The rain had ceased, but as they walked now across the bridge, clouds hung low over the twin towers and gargoyles of Notre-Dame, not far off on the north bank of the river, and over the hoary candle-snuffer turrets of La Conciergerie, massive on the bank behind them.

Not yet had the trees along the cobbled *quais* put forth a bud, and their bare branches were as dark as the river that in the waning afternoon divided its current with a white frill of foam about the stone embankment, lifting like a ship's prow, of the Ile Saint-Louis.

Despite the wine he had drunk at lunch, Poe's thoughts were as dark as the lowering clouds. He was troubled by the interview he had witnessed at Neuilly.

Until then, he had taken it for granted that this young man, ten years his junior, walking now at his side—this young poet with his striking good looks and refined affectations, who so generously was sharing his roof with a penniless stranger—had money, had family resources from which to finance his carelessly opulent way of life.

Poe had been disabused of this notion by the interview he had witnessed among the dusty, pink-taped dossiers in Monsieur Ancelle's bureau at Neuilly. Too often, in the past, Poe had had to seek refuge under roofs where he was not wanted, eat food he was begrudged. The pride secreted in the core of his being had been scarred repeatedly by the mean stabs of necessity. The hole in the glove, the shoe that leaked, the frayed sleeve cuff, the touch of mange in the nap of the hat, the handkerchief grayed by washings and indifferently smooth from pressing on window-panes—such small shames of paltry poverty went ill with a conviction of fire in the soul.

How different, this interlude—this oasis in life—with Charles Baudelaire! Poe had felt curiously at ease with the young poet in his fine apartment in the Hôtel Lauzun, though his alias had begun to weigh upon his conscience as he divined that, latent in Baudelaire, there was something more than a mother's pampered boy, a dandy in pink silk gloves.

A dozen times Poe had been on the point of confessing his imposture. But poverty bred fear. If his confession were ill taken, he would be without subsistence. He would be on the streets, with no shelter but these dank old bridges over the icy Seine.

He glanced down, troubled, over the parapet at the flutter of foam about the stone prow of the Ile Saint-Louis, and remembered a framed slogan in pokerwork which he had seen hanging on the wall of a quayside café overlooking this river:

"On est mieux ici qu'en face!"

"Did you say something, Henri?" Baudelaire asked.

Poe realized that he had muttered the trenchant sentiment half audibly.

"Just a thought that crossed my mind," he said. " 'Better here than—' " He motioned a black-gloved hand at the river.

"A gay thought," said Baudelaire, "to help digest a good lunch!"

"Such is my temperament," said Poe. "I'm not really a soldier, Charles."

"So what are you?" asked Baudelaire, swinging his gold-knobbed stick airily as they walked.

Close ahead now were the gray stone walls and the many windows of the Hôtel Lauzun. Behind them lay refuge. Fires glowed cozily on the hearths in there. Soon the lamps would be lit, the rich velour curtains drawn to shut out the cold river and the dark of night.

"What are you, Henri?" Baudelaire asked again, as they walked across the cobbles toward the vast old warren that had sheltered many heads renowned in the annals of France.

The resolve which Poe had been trying to pump up subsided abjectly. Tomorrow, he thought. Tomorrow, most certainly. Meanwhile—

"I'm an undertaker," he said.

Baudelaire checked, staring. Two tumbrils, with horses glooming into nosebags, were standing before the doorway of the old *hôtel*, and two men with hobnailed boots and green baize aprons were carrying out a handsome bookcase.

"What's this?" said Baudelaire. He hastened forward, shouting, "You there—just a minute!"

The removal men paused, bearing the bookcase between them with its shelves uppermost, still packed with books bound beautifully in tooled morocco.

"That's *my* bookcase!" Baudelaire was incredulous. "And my books!" He looked at the furniture already laden on the tumbril. "My God! My furniture! Henri, these frightful ruffians are making off with my goods and chattels!"

"What does this mean?" Poe demanded of the removers, though he had a sinking premonition.

"Distraining order," replied one of the stalwarts.

Baudelaire pointed imperiously with his stick. "Put down that bookcase immediately!"

"You'll have to talk to the bailiff, monsieur. He's inside."

The men heaved the bookcase up onto the tumbril. The other tumbril was already loaded.

"This passes belief!" said Baudelaire, stunned.

He gave Poe a pale look, then ran to the doorway. A third baize-aproned man was coming out with a roll of carpet bending over each shoulder.

"Good God," said Baudelaire, "my Aubusson!"

He ran into the wide hall, Poe stalking after him. The concierge hurried out from his loge, wringing consternation from his hands.

"Monsieur Baudelaire—I tried to stop them—"

Baudelaire hurried past him, Poe following with a heavy heart. Since the disquieting revelations at the interview with Monsieur Ancelle, he had had an uneasy feeling that, with his greater experience of man's inhumanity to man, he had now a truer appreciation of Baudelaire's financial circumstances than had Baudelaire himself.

In the salon of the apartment, a stout man wearing a Sergent de Ville type of hat failed to remove it as he handed Baudelaire a grim-looking document which Baudelaire took distractedly, looking in horror about the ravaged room.

"My tapestries! My Chinese wall panels! My lacquered screens! My curtains! Look at this, Henri—look! These monsters have peeled the very underfelt from the floor!"

"On petition," said the Sergent de Ville, "of all such several and sundry creditors as heretofore was served upon you by due process, Monsieur Baudelaire, and therein named and enumerated in accordance."

"I take no notice of such things," said Baudelaire.

"The bailiff," said the sergeant, drawing himself up, "is not mocked."

Baudelaire strode into the adjoining rooms. His footsteps echoed on bare floors. Doors banged hollowly. His voice cried despair from the void: "My wardrobe!"

"So much the worse!" said the sergeant to Poe—and departed.

Poe looked about the bare room, forlorn in the fading daylight from the curtainless windows. *Déjà vu!* How often had he known such disasters! It seemed to him that he carried poverty about with him, a blight that infected everything and everyone he touched. Now, even Baudelaire—who, like every young poet, idealized the gutter as a rich source of literary inspiration, but, less experienced than Poe, would find its reality unbearable.

Poe looked at Baudelaire with pity as he strode back into the room in his purple-lined cape and canary waistcoat, with his gold-knobbed stick in his hand and his silk hat on the back of his head, his eyes dark with stupefaction at the pillaging of his premises.

"My clothes," he said. "Gone, every stitch! Henri, they've stripped the whole place. How can they do these things? The wretches have even taken our beds!"

He strode, still only half-believing, to the windows.

Poe, in his caped greatcoat and towering hat, stood watching the younger man for a moment, then moved to his side.

Silhouetted there together against the naked panes, they stood gazing out.

Melancholy twilight deepened in the room.

"Do you still say, Henri," asked Baudelaire, " '*On est mieux ici qu'en face*'? "

Ten

Dispossessed, they glazed out gloomily at the river flowing darkly, bearing patches of ice on its current, under the venerable arches of the bridge.

Piled high with a poet's possessions, the fatal tumbrils lumbered onto the bridge, the stout man walking beside them, supervisory—Nemesis, in a functional hat, by warrant of the Paris *Parquet*.

"Every article," mourned Baudelaire, "selected for its elegance and distinction—"

Poe put a comforting hand on Baudelaire's shoulder.

"The times I've had in this apartment!" said Baudelaire. "Roger de Beauvoir himself had to admit that my parties were inimitable—the most fashionably vicious in contemporary Paris."

"My poor friend," said Poe, "what can I say to you?"

As he spoke, a tapping of heels became audible, rapidly approaching. They echoed louder on bare boards—and stopped abruptly.

"Well, this is a fine thing!" a voice said. "A fine thing indeed, this is!"

Poe and Baudelaire turned. Across the room, so barren and stark with the doors of its wall cupboards yawning open, stood a figure in a coat and Muscovite hat of white fur, hands in a white fur muff, face a dusk-dark blur, almost invisible in the fading light.

"Have they taken everything?" asked Jeanne Duval.

"The very shirts off my back," said Baudelaire bitterly.

"So it's not much good mooning around in here. You have some clothes at my place, Charles." Pearly teeth and whites of eyes flashed momentarily in the shadow-blur of her face. "You'd better come!"

She turned and went.

Poe and Baudelaire looked at each other. Desolation filled Poe's heart. His throat ached, but he swallowed the lump in it and forced a smile.

"So, Charles—the parting of the ways," he said, with ghastly bravado. *"C'est la vie!"*

He held out his hand. Baudelaire took it and, holding it hard, looked searchingly into Poe's eyes for a moment, then drew his arm under his own and clamped it tight.

"My American," said Baudelaire.

With Poe's arm linked, firmly pinioned, in Baudelaire's, they walked together from the room, following the receding click of Jeanne's footsteps.

As the last daylight faded, nothing was left in the plundered room except, on the shelf of a cupboard, a stack of old news-print—*The Dollar Newspaper* and other transatlantic periodicals.

Jeanne's apartment was not far away.

It was on the fifth floor of one of the tall old narrow houses that looked down on the leafless trees in the tiny, triangular

Place Dauphine, near the oldest of the Seine bridges, the Pont-Neuf, guarded by its equestrian statue of Henri IV.

At the expense of Baudelaire in the affluent days before his style had been crippled by the prudent arrangement that had placed what remained of his patrimony in the trust administered by Monsieur Ancelle, Jeanne had furnished her diminutive apartment to her own taste.

It smacked of the gorgeous East.

Crimson hangings draped bell-shape from the ceiling and quilted to the walls by padded studs gave to the tiny salon the air of a tented pavilion erected for the concubines of Saladin accompanying him, for his comfort, on campaign against the infidel.

Boat-shaped lamps of the harem type, wherein flickered the flame of wicks in perfumed oil, stood on pedestals of ivory and ebony, and cast a glow over the Persian carpet and on the prayer rugs and silken cushions that graced the ottomans and divans.

Doors, those crude appurtenances of the Occident, had been banished by Jeanne. In their place hung beaded curtains. One of these gave on to a tiny lobby. Another concealed the voluptuous appointments of Jeanne's bedroom. A third dangled from the arch of a recess in which were hooks bearing garments, including a West Point greatcoat and a tall beaver hat.

Here, under shelves laden with portmanteaux, hatboxes, vases and samovars, the untimely guest, Baudelaire's American, lay drowsing on a low couch which had been arranged for his temporary accommodation in the emergency which had all but put him on the cruel streets of Paris.

The ballet at the Théâtre du Panthéon had closed to make way for an incursion of acrobats, dwarfs, conjurers, sword-swallowers and performing poodles, and Jeanne herself was without gainful employment. In the circumstances, the *ménage à trois* had lost no time in transmuting its collective problems into the smoke which drifted now in acrid swaths about the flickering lamps.

The smoke had come from long-stemmed pipes of bamboo

lying on a low coffee table of tulipwood inset with medallions of mother-of-pearl. On the beaten brass of the tabletop were also a cloisonné saucer holding greasy black pellets of raw opium and a pair of tweezers, with a small censer bowl containing a handful of charcoal redly smoldering.

Among the cushions of the ottoman beside the table Jeanne reclined in a caftan embroidered by Kurdish fingers, her own slim fingers idle on the strings of a lute. Baudelaire, in a royal blue robe gold-encrusted with a baleful dragon, half-reclined beside her on the ottoman. He toyed with her toes and a bangle on her ankle, but his eyes roamed to a gorilla head that bared jungle fangs at him from a quilted wall niche.

It annoyed him that she had kept that damned object. Why had she done it? The feral grin mocked his secret shame.

"You cruel bitch," he murmured to Jeanne's closed eyes. She half-opened them, glimmering amber up at him. "Um!"

"Nothing," said Baudelaire, "my supple artiste—my ebon Thespian. Nothing, my sweetling."

Jeanne smiled vaguely, cloudy from opium, and drew her lazy fingers over the strings of the lute.

Its crystal note drifted to her house guest recumbent in his recess, to which he had retired partly from the motive of tact seemly in a lodger and partly because his head was so swimming from opiate fumes that he had been unable to remain even approximately upright.

At the note of the lute, his eyes half opened. It was hot in his nook. Poe was wearing a rich red opium-smoking jacket, Berber slippers and a Byronically frilled shirt, all borrowed from Baudelaire, and sweat plastered his thinning curls to his high, pale brow.

He was vaguely aware of a familiar feeling, a subtle sinking and swaying and gentle corkscrewing of the resting place on which he lay. Vertical stripes of faint light and shadow flickered on his own greatcoat and hat dangling so close above him that, as he slowly turned his head, the skirts of the greatcoat lightly brushed his brow.

Drunk again, he thought drearily. Where was he this time?

He frowned, trying to remember; but the brass vessel he cloudily perceived on a shelf was difficult to account for. A samovar? Some vague recollection of war with Russia stirred in his mind. He remembered snow, a blizzard, the glow of a bivouac fire, the body of some captured spy soaked in oil and hung, flaming and gyrating in the wind from the tundras, in clanking chains on a high gallows.

Russian barbarism, he thought. Again the note of plucked strings floated to his ears. Balalaikas? He was not drunk, then. He was a prisoner, dying of wounds in some casualty-clearing station on the steppes north of the Vistula, while the victorious Russian hordes celebrated with Tartar dances about their million cooking fires dotting the illimitable wastes of snow all around.

"Water," he croaked huskily. "Water."

But only a note or two from the balalaikas answered him. Closing his weary eyes, he resigned himself to death—and here to him, fallen on this foreign field, came the wraith of Virginia, her face pale and grieving in its frame of ringlets as she beckoned him home.

His lips, parched under his moustache, moved, whispering to her, "Oh, lady dear, hast though no fear?/ Why and wherefore hast thou come here?"

Faintly, again, from the Cossack bivouacs sounded the note of the balalaika.

"Sure thou art come o'er far-off seas,/ A wonder to these garden trees—"

He found himself walking now in a place of mossed and leaning headstones, through rank grass, dark yew trees, and the sodden, dead heads of sunflowers nodding in mournful unison as he followed with outstretched, pleading hands the wraith of Virginia.

"Strange is thy pallor! Strange thy dress!/ And all this solemn silentness—"

He stumbled after the pitiful wraith as it levitated through an opening, hung dankly around with poison ivy, into a crypt lit with a spectral glow emanating from no identifiable source. A slab of stone leaned against the roof of a stone catafalque carven with crumbling coats-of-arms. Bats hanging head down from the roof of the crypt unhooked themselves and flickered blindly about him as the wraith subsided ethereally into the catafalque.

He stood looking down at her, so beautiful, so young. Poor Virginia! She beckoned to him, her final gesture, then slowly closed her eyes.

"My love, she sleeps! Oh, may her sleep,/ As it is lasting, so be deep!"

He climbed into the catafalque and lay down at her side. With a hand which already he could feel stiffening into time-defying marble, he made a strange, cabalistic sign known only to the inmost circle of the illuminati. Thus conjured, the stone slab leaning against the catafalque began slowly to elevate itself, tilting, grinding heavily against the edge of the catafalque.

Poe gazed up with glazing eyes at the massive lid impending hugely above himself and Virginia. With waning strength, he clasped her icy hand as the heavy slab of lid hovered obliquely over them, awaiting the final command—which Poe, with rigor mortis beginning to congeal his lips under his moustache, uttered with his last, expiring breath:

"Soft may the worms about us creep!"

Obedient, the slab fell into place with a thud that sealed the catafalque in eternal dark.

Unaware of fatalities in their house guest's recess off the salon, Jeanne and Baudelaire had retired to the bedroom. Under the draperies tented in graceful folds from the apex of the high valance, they lay facing each other on the wide bed which clutched the carpet with gilded lion claws.

"Enchantress with the bee-stung mouth," murmured Baudelaire, kissing it. "Lips sweeter than Nubian honey in the tawny shade of lost oases—"

They were naked, a study in black and white, Baudelaire propped gracefully on one elbow at her side, his other hand intimately caressing her.

"Take me," said Jeanne, in a whisper—for opium, to which she was long inured, seemed to have on her a stimulating effect, and her eyes glimmered up their amber invitation at him through long lashes.

"The snow-white camel," mused Baudelaire, half-aloud, as he brushed her nipples with his silkily bearded lips, "kneels at her command. . . ."

Though it was months ago that Jeanne had introduced him to opium, he still was more vulnerable than she to its insidious effects, and it called forth from him a certain amount of effort to get himself arranged comfortably on top of her, supporting his weight on his elbows and, cupping her face in pale fingers, lightly kissing her eyelids.

"*La très-chère,*" he murmured, "*était nue,/ Et, connaissant mon coeur—*"

"Don't talk," she breathed. "I thirst. Come, slake me, Charles."

But Beaudelaire's trouble, known to them alone, and often contended with on nights of love and disappointment, was now again upon him—and, even as he strove with it, he clung to the lifeline of healing words.

"*Elle n'avait gardé que ses bijoux sonores—*"

"Hush," she breathed—and, looking up at him, smoothed back the lock of hair that fell slanting across his brow. "*Mon chou—*"

But his head bowed forward, in defeat, to her shoulder. And with a sudden lithe movement of her scented, slippery body, she rippled out from beneath him, reversing their positions; she now on him, smiling encouragement down at him, her teeth and the whites of her eyes aflash in the dark beauty of her face and the loosened cloud of her hair.

"Like this," she whispered. "Come, Charles—"

"Ah, *non,*" he gasped, despairing. "Forgive me."

He rolled out from under her, and from the silken sheets, and snatched up his robe from the carpet to conceal the wound he had come by in Mauritius.

Jeanne, with a sigh, lay back upon the pillows. She looked up at him, saying helplessly, *"Pauvre* Charles—"

He drew tight the girdle of his robe, shaking his head as he backed barefoot to the bead curtain hanging in the doorway.

"Mon pauvre," Jeanne said gently.

She groped for the sheet to cover her beauty, and lay gazing up unseeingly at the apex of the draped valance, as, to Baudelaire's going, the beads of the curtain in the doorway clicked and swayed.

In the little salon, the lighted wicks floated, flickering, in the perfumed oil of the boat-shaped lamps. Baudelaire, rubbing at his face and hair with shaking hands, prowled the carpet and raged inwardly against Aupick, who had imposed on him that voyage that had ended at Mauritius. And what an end, good Christ!

He looked at the opium pipes on the low table. The charcoal still glowed a sullen red, loosing wisps of smoke, in the censer bowl. Suddenly he could no longer abide, in solitude, the poisoned gnawings of his shames and memories.

"Henri!" he called. *"Henri!"*

Stirrings, creakings, moans of strangulation, sounded through the bead curtain that masked the house guest's recess.

Baudelaire stood staring at the gorilla head, grinning its jungle virility at him from the wall niche. He seized the head by the sparse hair gummed to its papier-mâché scalp, and held it aloft.

"Give me," he bitterly invoked the jungle grin, "the lust of anthropoid apes! Erect me a horn to belittle rhinos and shame unicorns!"

He clapped the head on over his own, the flanges of the gorilla head resting on the shoulders of his dragon-encrusted robe.

The curtain strings of Poe's recess rattled. The house guest emerged, blinking, wavering on his slippered feet from the vertigo of opium and nightmares.

Baudelaire turned on him a stare that was lost in hollow eye sockets sunken under black bone ridges. Bared canines gleamed.

Poe drew back from them with a haggard look.

"A pipe," said the gorilla, through brutish fangs. "A pipe, for God's sake, Henri!"

Poe passed a tremulous hand over his face.

"All that we see or seem," he faltered, "is but a dream within a dream."

"Hamlet?" asked Baudelaire, decapitating himself.

He tossed the gorilla head onto the ottoman, and tossed himself after it.

Poe stood looking about him with a distraught expression.

Baudelaire, wilted among the cushions, lay with his fingertips pressed to his throbbing temples.

"Pipes, Henri," he said. "Let's seek Nirvana!"

"Willingly," said Poe, making a strong effort to pull himself together.

His knees bending under him, he sank slowly to the carpet, and there, cross-legged in a posture reminiscent of the lotus sit, he fumbled between the cord frogs of his smoking jacket, found his handkerchief. Fanning the charcoal with it, he became aware of a gap in his new-found and congenial domestic circle.

"Where's Jeanne?" he asked.

Baudelaire waved a languid hand in the general direction of Jeanne's bedchamber. Falling, the hand encountered her lute, sharing the ottoman with himself and the gorilla head. He plucked a nostalgic note from the lute, murmuring, " 'If music be the food of love—' "

" 'Play on!' " said Poe—then gave the lute a puzzled glance, vaguely associating it with some different instrument recently heard by him somewhere or other.

"Play on?" said Baudelaire. He let fall the lute. "No, Henri, no love songs—whether of Illyria or Mauritius."

The charcoal in the censer bowl began to glow, with faint crackling sounds, and Poe, with the tweezers, picked up from the saucer a pellet of opium.

"Mauritius?" he said. "Where the dodo died, under the clubs of hungry mariners?"

"In a welter," murmured Baudelaire, "of blood and feathers. Feathers of the dodo, Henri—and *my* blood."

"Yours, Charles?" Poe held the pellet in the tweezers close over the glow of the charcoal.

"A beautiful island, Henri—ringed by a wide blue sea, under a tropical sun."

Greasily, blackly, the pellet of opium bubbled over the charcoal. Baudelaire lay silent, gazing up unseeingly at the tented ceiling drapes. Poe dropped the pellet into the bowl of one of the bamboo pipes, with the tweezers placed on the pellet a sliver of red-hot charcoal. He puffed at the pipe until smoke came. Then, holding the smoke in his mouth, he held out the pipe to Baudelaire, who sucked smoke from it and handed the pipe back to Poe.

Baudelaire exhaled the smoke and a sigh.

"Beautiful island," he said; "beautiful women. Idle women—garrison ladies—officers' wives, officials' wives—restless and bored with themselves in the ennui of long, hot afternoons."

Vaguely, his head swimming as he toasted another pellet over the charcoal in the censer bowl, Poe felt that what he was hearing was a revelation of some importance.

"There was one, Henri," Baudelaire murmured, "creamy-bosomed as a rose full-blown, who made welcome a stranger—a young stranger from Paris—self-marooned, poor idiot. *Que voulez-vous?*"

He laughed briefly, without mirth.

"La très-chère était nue, et, connaissant mon coeur,/Elle n'avait gardé que ses bijoux sonores,/Dont le riche attirail lui donnait l'air vainqueur/Qu'ont dans leurs jours heureux les esclaves des Mores."

"Exquisite lines, Charles," Poe murmured, handing Baudelaire another pipe.

Baudelaire sucked in the smoke.

"Sonnet for a siesta," he said, returning the pipe. "*Siesta for Two*. While the servants in their compound slept—the officials snored under the punkahs in their *bureau*—the officers in their mess clicked billiard balls."

Poe dribbled smoke slowly from his mouth and stared at the glow of the charcoal in the censer bowl.

"Over all the island," said Baudelaire, "only the tremble of the heat currents. Not a frond, Henri, astir in the airless hush; no sound but the seething of the crickets in the dust. And the throb of her heart against mine, in the hot, dim room—behind the drawn jalousies." He lifted a hand, and let it fall.

"*Et, alors,*" said Baudelaire, "one day—*bang!* He kicked out the lock of the door—her husband in his righteous wrath and white regimentals with medals, and a loaded swagger cane in his hand. And he struck, Henri—with malice aforethought—*just* where a naked man is most vulnerable. You know?"

"Smoke, Charles," said Poe, handing him a pipe.

Baudelaire sucked in smoke from it.

"Her name," he said slowly, "was Héloïse. D'you think, Henri, that the gods laughed?"

"They were jealous of your talent," said Poe. "Take comfort from that, Charles, not from—"

"My lady of dusk and amber?" Baudelaire said, with a wave of his hand toward Jeanne's bedchamber.

"Nothing can cripple talent," Poe said, out of his deep, corroding knowledge, "except—poverty. I've seen now its leprous hand hover over your bright youth. Charles, take care! These debts—"

"Oh, those! I'll deal with them. A day will come."

"Compound interest, Charles—the amoeba that reproduces itself—world without end, amen."

"What can I do? What's left of my capital's tied up."

"It should be used *now,* to free you of debt before it crushes you. Charles, I know something of these things."

"Tell it to Aupick," Baudelaire said bitterly.

"If he should die?" said Poe. The fumes swam in his head, as he held another pellet in the tweezers over the charcoal.

"I could get around my mother," said Baudelaire, "and Monsieur Ancelle. I could touch my capital." He pounded the ottoman with his fist. "Oh, God *damn* General Aupick!"

"He stands square in your way," said Poe. "And I, too, have a bone to pick with him. He blocked my road to Poland."

He handed a pipe, after sucking smoke from it, to Baudelaire.

"Henri," Baudelaire murmured, "revolution brews. Who knows? A Paris street mob, mad with looted wine, storming the Invalides! A stray bullet—"

He sucked smoke, seeing General Aupick fall, riddled with bullet holes, on a balcony above the Invalides courtyard, as the roaring crowd rushed in, overthrowing the cannons, smashing the limbers.

"Revolution," said Poe. "A chancy weapon—unpredictable. Your crisis, Charles, is *now!*" Plots swam behind his great plotster's brow, dank with sweat. Exquisite ingenuities combined for him in irresistible patterns. Not since he had thrown down his pen on the completed manuscript of "The Gold Bug" had he felt such confidence, so sure a sense of intellectual mastery.

"Charles," he said, "give me twenty-four hours. I'll make a plan—and pay my debt to you."

"Your debt?" said Baudelaire, raising himself on an elbow.

Poe, the bamboo pipe wisping smoke in his hand, looked up, his face Mephistophelean in the glow from the charcoal.

"I owe you," he said, with the clairvoyance of opium, *"one perfect murder!"*

Eleven

It was not yet daybreak, but the moon had long set. Over the Alpine peaks looming high and snow-covered above the wide-eaved roof of the Auberge du Pont de Lodi, near Grenoble, the stars were beginning to pale.

Warmly wrapped against the cold, Kate Casteign was standing in the wooden gallery which, roofed, ran around three sides of the inn's cobbled courtyard. Her gloved hands on the balustrade, she looked down at lanthorns jogging to and fro across the courtyard as the inn servants stacked the travelers' luggage for loading.

The cry of a coaching horn rang out, and the Paris mail coach came lumbering in under the arch. The hoofs of the six horses at a walk, with ostlers clinging to the heads of the leaders, struck blue sparks from the cobbles, and the horses' breath smoked on the frosted air.

This, Kate thought, was going to be a marvelous day for traveling—and, excited by the prospect, she turned, opened a door behind her, went into the coffee room.

Here, around a blazing fire, huddled her fellow travelers, sipping coffee and gnawing bread with the glassy-eyed automatism of the barely awakened.

"It's here!" Kate brightly informed the moribund company. "The coach has just come around from the stables!"

"As if we didn't know," said Lady Casteign acidly. "That horn would wake the dead."

Her traveling veil rolled up to the brim of her widow's bonnet, Lady Casteign was drinking, not coffee, but an English gentlewoman's obligatory tea. The tea basket containing the necessary impedimenta stood open on the table before her, together with her strapped-up rug roll with umbrella handles protruding from each end. She helped herself to an Abernethy biscuit from the biscuit barrel in the basket and, munching, checked up on how much tea remained in the tea caddy painted with enchanting views of Balmoral Castle.

The other travelers began to stand up slowly, reluctant to drag themselves away from the fire.

"Monsieur Goubillon," said Kate, "you promised to change seats with me, remember? So that I could sit on top beside the coachman."

Goubillon, a tall, sad, raw-boned youth, a student of philosophy bound for the University of Paris, with a perpetual dewdrop on the tip of his nose, bowed agreement.

"*A votre service, mademoiselle,*" he said and, carrying his carpet bag, moved away, sniffing.

"If he sits inside, Kate," said Lady Casteign, "and sniffs at me sadly all day, it will be the last straw."

"He'll be just fine," said Kate, who could hardly wait to get to Paris. "Are you ready, Mother?"

She closed the lid of the tea basket. Lady Casteign promptly opened it again.

"I haven't finished with my cup yet," she said, with asperity. "I shall be ready when I have recruited myself, Kate, and not before. What with being tossed about miserably on that awful Italian ship in the Straits of Bonifacio, and now this interminable coach journey, I feel by no means myself."

"Only a few days more," said Kate. "Oh, Mother, we *must* get to Paris before Henry leaves for the battles in Poland! The coachman tells me we should enter Paris by the Porte d'Italie on Friday evening."

"If his horses don't drop dead or his wheels come off," said Lady Casteign. "And if we surmount these hazards, which seems improbable after the mishaps of yesterday, has it occurred to you that we have no idea where to *look* for Henry Duprez in Paris?"

"Eleanor Gerrard may know," said Kate. "We'll go straight to the address she wrote to me from."

"En voiture!" sounded the bawl of the coachman. *"En voiture, messieurs les voyageurs!"*

"Eleanor may well have left Paris," said Lady Casteign, closing the tea basket; "eloped, very likely, with her peculiar companion, this Sir Bertram Moon she spoke of in her letter. American girls are uncontrolled and headstrong."

"I shall find Henry somehow," said Kate, "if I have to follow him to the ends of the earth."

"You would be more useful," said Lady Casteign, "if you followed the inn bumpkins and chivvied them so that they put *all* our things on the coach." She added, as Kate went off to chivvy the bumpkins, "Ah, good morning to you, landlord."

"Milady has slept well?" inquired the landlord, raising his Swiss-type hat, which had a tall feather at the back.

"As well as can be expected," said Lady Casteign, "when half one's joints have been sprung by the coach's jolting."

"Progress speeds upon us, milady," said the landlord, as he picked up Lady Casteign's tea basket and rug roll. " 'Tis said that tracks are being laid to Grenoble for the coming of the iron horse." He escorted her out onto the gallery. "Ah, see—the sky lightens over the snow peaks. I predict fair weather for you today on Napoleon's *route nationale.*"

"A glorious highway," said Lady Casteign. "It's a pity he can't return to have the potholes seen to."

"*Madame, je vous en prie!*" bawled the coachman from his box. "*Dépêchez-vous!*"

In no mood to jostle herself so early in the day, Lady Casteign descended the wooden steps from the gallery at her own dignified gait.

"Get *in,* Mother!" cried Kate from her perch beside the coachman. "The horses are impatient!"

The landlord holding open the coach door for her, Lady Casteign mounted unhurriedly into the vehicle, while the hapless ostlers scuffled and reeled as they clung to the horses' tossing heads.

"*Bon voyage,* milady," said the landlord, thudding the door shut after her.

"That remains to be seen," said Lady Casteign, with a pinched smile. "*Adieu,* mine host."

The coach trundled out under the arch onto the highway.

"*En avant!*" bawled the coachman. "*Allons-y!*"

His whip cracked. The ostlers sprang back from the horses' heads. The team surged into its collars. The Paris Mail rumbled off, jingling and rattling, and, gathering speed, receded rapidly along the highway as dawn began to brighten over the snow-capped Alpine summits.

The postilion, perched on his dickey seat, raised his horn to his lips, and the long blare floated back, fading, to the landlord and his merry bumpkins at the Auberge du Pont de Lodi.

In Paris, on the afternoon of that same day, Baudelaire and his American were walking through the Luxembourg Gardens on their way to the *Infirmerie des Indigents,* the Paris paupers' hospital.

Despite the reduced state of their joint finances, it was not their intention to apply for admission for themselves, though in fact many men of letters had found it convenient, even imperative, to end their cheerless days in that institution.

But the purpose of Baudelaire and his American was to further the enterprise they had in hand to encompass the downfall of General Aupick, and Baudelaire was apologizing again for his own unmanly doubts about certain aspects of the matter.

"It's my mother, Henri," he said. "God alone knows why, but she has an affection for the General. To me personally, of course, the idea of murdering him appeals inordinately. The exquisite emotion attendant upon the act itself would transcend, by the sense it would bestow of revealed potentiality for creative evil, one's response to one's first orgasm, however induced."

"You speak as a poet, Charles," said Poe. "The soldier, on the other hand, once he's slain his first man, finds that his response to the achievement, so keenly anticipated during his recruit training, soon loses its edge through mere repetition. The mystery of Being, acutely enough perceived by him as he dispatches his initial victim through a crack in Eternity, yields to the mundane geometry of the *Manual of Arms,* which contains no chapter touching on the mooted immortality of the soul."

"Extraordinary," said Baudelaire.

"Thus," said Poe, "the soldier's emotional arteries—so to call them—quickly harden into mere professionalism. Of this, there are two types. The more common is the General Aupick type—rigid, mindless, uninventive, essentially Prussian. The rarer type, more suited to high command, tends to combine agile adaptability with analytical ingenuity. An inhuman type, that, Charles—of which," Poe added with a shrug, "I detect intimations in myself."

"I can't say I've felt that about you, Henri," Baudelaire admitted, "though I must say your murder plan is ingenious— dazzlingly so! But I believe ingenuity's a characteristic of your countrymen as a whole?"

"How else could we have created a nation?" said Poe.

"I read, not long ago," said Baudelaire, "a tale in the original American. It was called 'The Gold Bug.' "

Poe all but stopped dead in his tracks.

"I was at first amused, then quite absorbed," said Baudelaire, "by its sheer ingenuity. But your plan for murdering Aupick, my dear Henri, has a stealthy intricacy that far outshines your compatriot's tale. Ah, if only it weren't for this complicating factor of my mother!"

Baudelaire's voice, continuing to talk as they walked on together between the statues and trees of the Luxembourg Gardens, misty in the gray afternoon, reached Poe through the thin cry of a bugle.

It was a bugle at Fort Moultrie, on the tip of Sullivan's Island near Charleston, South Carolina, and the summons of the bugle rang in the ears of Pvt. Edgar A. Perley, who chose to ignore it.

Sharp remarks had been addressed to him by a hard-eyed lieutenant at the morning muster, and Pvt. Perley, scorning an imposed fatigue of removing night soil in the latrine cart on his road to glory, had wandered off to nurse his resentment in the solitude of the surrounding sandhills.

Dotted with clumps of myrtle and palmetto and cried over sadly by tidewater birds, the dunes rolled away under the sun to where distant rollers broke on the shore in a seething line of white.

In his country's proud uniform—none too well fitting, and inspiringly referred to in War Department documents as an "issue of public clothing"—Pvt. Perley contemplated the seascape with hollow eyes.

The distant bugle cried to him in vain, for his hatred of life in Fort Moultrie had given way to other thoughts—thoughts of the buccaneers who once, long ago, had careened their ships, barbecued their meat, buried their loot, gambled, caroused and murdered each other, here among the low dunes of Sullivan's Island.

He noticed a beetle crawling on the sand at his feet. Some-how, it fitted in with his thoughts. He picked it up. It had markings on it that resembled a human skull.

A solitary figure in the sandy waste, with the gulls crying, his defaulter's ears wilfully deaf to the distant bugle, he stood watching the death's-head bug crawl on the palm of his hand, in the sunshine of Sullivan's Island.

"So, with the feeling my mother unfortunately has for General Aupick—well, you do understand, Henri?"

Tidewater bird cries, pealing bugle, Pvt. Edgar A. Perley—all dissolved into the past. Classical statues and formally barbered trees in the misty light of a Paris afternoon resurrected them-selves for Poe as he walked with Baudelaire on the broad pathway through the Luxembourg Gardens.

"Of course, Charles," he said mechanically.

"Between my mother and myself," Baudelaire explained, "there's a—how shall I say?—a rapport that might be affected to some extent if she should find out I had helped murder her husband."

"Women are strange," said Poe, thinking it stranger yet that Charles Baudelaire should have read "The Gold Bug," written years after its first nebulous conception; read it, more-over, with respect and admiration, though little dreaming at whose side he walked.

"My feeling, I admit," said Baudelaire, "is sickly sentimen-tality. I despise myself for it, as I'm sure you must do."

"I?" Poe said. "Despise *you?*"

The weirdness of the situation overwhelmed him. Baude-laire's praise of "The Gold Bug" had warmed Poe as a beaker of mulled wine might warm a beggar on a cold night in a long winter of neglect. No one, he knew now, walked the earth whose praise he more coveted than that of this pink-gloved young poet who was so much more than the sum of his affectations. He must be told. He must know the truth.

"Despise?" said Poe again. "No, Charles—no! I—"

"Thank heaven you understand," said Baudelaire. "Henri, my affinity! I hate to leave Aupick unmurdered, but the ingenuity of your alternative plan is beyond praise!"

The moment, Poe realized, was not after all just right for selfish personal revelations. Baudelaire's mind was entirely taken up with the immediate issue, the undoing of General Aupick. Other moments would come, thought Poe—more appropriate moments.

"Simplicity, Charles," he said, "is the secret of success. A decisive maneuver will always be found, on analysis, to have been no more than a deft coordination of observed phenomena."

How else, thought Poe, had he come to write "The Gold Bug?"

Dismissing that thought, he went on. "In the matter at hand, we have (a) General Aupick's anticipated appointment to an ambassadorship; (b) your friend Eugène Sue has not only held officer's rank on active service but is also a qualified medical man—"

"Not now in practice," said Baudelaire.

"Immaterial," said Poe. "He knows the ropes. Now, then—(c) your friend Théophile Dondey, otherwise known as O'Neddy, wears glasses with thick corrective lenses."

"His eyes," said Baudelaire, "take on an uncanny enormity at times."

"So much the better," said Poe. "Now—(d) the evident stupidity and sycophancy of General Aupick's lawyer, Monsieur Ancelle, and the fact that he dines at regular intervals at the General Aupick's house."

"Every Thursday evening," said Baudelaire, "will find Monsieur Ancelle tucking his napkin into his collar at Number forty-four Rue Bourbon."

"Sheeplike adherence to habit," said Poe, "infallibly earmarks the good citizen, so-called, as likely prey for the freebooter. Now, then—juxtapose factors a, b, c and d in the situation, and maneuver accordingly, and the result, Charles, will be the liberation of your patrimony."

"You really think so?" asked Baudelaire, enchanted.

"Mathematically inevitable," said Poe.

"Inspired monster!" exclaimed Baudelaire. "Henri, you fiend, you can't imagine how much I esteem you!"

Impulsively, he linked arms with Poe.

"Baudelaire is making love to his American," piped a falsetto voice—"*en plein air* in the Luxembourg Gardens! Aren't they dreadful boys, Gaby?"

It was the composer, Armand Crespigny. He was wearing a tastefully embroidered tunic, baggy trousers tucked into red leather Turkish boots that curled back at the toes, and a kind of tailed turban. A fat white rat, led on a ribbon, partly crept, made sudden darts for liberation, and was partly dragged along behind him as he approached.

Passing ladies, noting the unhappy rodent, detoured around it, ostentatiously holding aside their skirts.

"What happened to your lobster?" asked Baudelaire.

"Ah, poor Crétin!" said the composer, crossing himself. "He kept making scraping noises when I was in all of a dither with my grace notes, so I snapped off his pretty feeler things. I'm sure he didn't suffer in the least, but he insisted on dying— looking at me quite hatefully with those stalky eyeballs of his. Isn't that sad? But there, now I have Gaby to comfort me."

"She looks fat," said Baudelaire.

"I'm afraid she's been incautious," said Crespigny. "If she has a litter, I shall do away with her—literally." He tittered. "Oh, what a quip!"

"Pass it on to your librettist," Baudelaire suggested.

"Alas, he has no sense of humor, Charles. Such a solemn fellow! He fails to grasp that judicious touches of harlequinade in an operatic work tend to elevate the poignancy of the spiritual passages. But tell me, dear boys—have you come to see the balloon go up?"

Poe and Baudelaire exchanged an involuntary glance.

"I've quite abandoned hope," said the composer, "and so has Gaby. But the aviators—see how manfully they persist in bobbing up and down at their pump, though the air—gas, ether, or whatever it is—keeps naughtily escaping!"

Nearby, in a circular clearing with stone seats around it, a fountain tossed its plume aloft. The falling water had congealed in icicles on the stone beard of Poseidon, whose uplifted trident of iron prongs seemed to be in ominous proximity to a large balloon.

Rapidly swelling, the netted balloon, with its bag painted all over with a map of the French provinces and their relevant produce of shellfish, grape bunches, cattle, swine, poultry and wine flagons, rose into the air above the fountain and jerked spasmodically at the pendent passenger basket.

Two aviators, warmly bescarved and tweed-clad, and watched by an admiring crowd eating roast chestnuts from a huckster's nearby barrow, were growing visibly warmer as they independently bent and straightened at each other over the twin handles of a plunger pump.

"Poor dears," said Crespigny, "they do try so hard!"

The aviators paused to glance up and shrewdly estimate the progress of corpulence in their aircraft, but it immediately began to hiss and, its map of gastronomic France shriveling and aging before their eyes, sank toward the forks of Poseidon's trident.

Hastily, the perspiring aviators resumed their Japaneselike exercise at the pump.

"Flight," said Crespigny; "man's fondest dream—I shall make it the subject of my next opera, it'll be *so* uplifting!'

"You'll need the personal experience," said Poe. "Charles, how stands the wind?"

"Due west, Henri," said Baudelaire, removing a pink silk glove to moisten a finger and hold it up; "northing a little."

"Cast off," said Poe.

"Anchor aweigh," said Baudelaire.

"We rise rapidly, Charles."

"All Paris spreads below us. How swiftly it dwindles, Henri!"

"The wind gusts ever more forcefully," said Poe. "Fair France speeds fast below us. *Oh*-oh, we sink a little! How're we placed for ballast?"

"We have Crespigny here, Henri."

"Let go ballast," Poe commanded.

"No! No!" screeched Crespigny.

"Ballast away," said Baudelaire. "Goodness, see how he falls!"

"Thus lightened," said Poe, "we fast regain altitude."

"How the gondola rocks, Henri! Are you keeping well?"

"So far," said Poe. He spied downward through the tunnel of his fingers. "What's that headland far below, lapped by the ocean at its priestly task? Here, Charles, take the telescope."

"Cape Finisterre," said Baudelaire, after a scrutiny. "So quickly left behind us! Look—look, Henri, there to the south'ard —a school of whales disporting!"

"Thar she blows!" said Poe, bluff Nantucketer. "We should have brought harpoons."

"We'll remember, another time," said Baudelaire. "Look, look—the Date Line! See how the mid-Atlantic rollers crash foaming on it!"

"Our bubble shadow," said Poe, "swoops over it into Yesterday."

"How time flies backward, Henri! No wonder I have so little to show for it!"

"Land, Charles! I smell the land!"

"Yes, yes, there it is, Henri—there to port!"

"So it was the port I smelt," said Poe. "Nought-eight was a vintage year. Yes, Charles, there lie the Azores."

"I fancy not," Baudelaire demurred. "More likely, the vex'd Bermoothes."

"In any case," said Poe, "clouds gather below us, hiding

all. Night's sable mantle speeds toward us over the rim of the world."

"How bright the stars shine now in the cosmos, Henri! Mark there the Pleiades! And how the Zodiac glows! Ah, poor Crespigny—if we hadn't had to sacrifice him, we could have taken him back the Crab for a pet!"

"Behold, Charles—the sun returns! The clouds part. Look there," said Poe, shading his eyes, "a coast ahead!"

"What ever coast can it be?" marveled Baudelaire.

"America," said Poe. "I know it well."

"Celestial pilot!" said Baudelaire admiringly. "What a homing instinct!" He pointed. "Look, look—a goodly city!"

"New York," said Poe proudly. "And the wind wanes. We sink."

"Those people, Henri—running like ants in the street!"

"We are observed, Charles! Look at all those upturned faces lining the Battery. And there—a sidewheeler belching black smoke as it casts off for Albany, its passengers staring up agog at us. A proud hour for us, Charles! A civic welcome no doubt awaits us."

"I'll put out our flags," said Baudelaire. "There, the Stars and Stripes and the Tricolor flutter bravely from our nether bulge."

"Heave on the starboard net ropes," said Poe, navigating, conning their approach ably. "We veer toward Staten Island! Ah, look—the coach of His Honor the Mayor coming with horses at a wild gallop to collect us for our triumphal entry into the city. A true New York welcome!"

"Will the American ladies," asked Baudelaire anxiously, "receive us with thrown flowers and warm embraces?"

"Undoubtedly," said Poe. "This is a great day! Be sure that the compositors of the New York *Daily Mirror* are hastily setting up type in upper case: LAFAYETTE ARGONAUTS ARRIVE—FRANCO-AMERICAN AVIATORS' INCREDIBLE FLIGHT—ATLANTIC SPANNED IN THREE DAYS!"

"The anchor, Henri, the anchor!"

"Anchor down—and dragging! Hold tight now, Charles—hold tight!"

They staggered against each other, shoulder to shoulder, as the gondola struck.

"Safe!" Baudelaire gasped. "Terra firma!"

"Hoboken," said Poe.

"And so they open the Air Age for us, Gaby," said Crespigny to his rat. "Such cruel fellows—but *so* intrepid! Sons of the Sun God!"

Earthbound again, Poe's exhilaration at his return home in spectacular triumph ebbed from him.

He said, with a homesick sigh, "Just a touch of judicious harlequinade."

The small crowd of spectators around the anchored balloon sagging with exhaustion above the trident prongs of stony-eyed, ice-bearded Poseidon had transferred their attention to the more interesting performance of Poe and Baudelaire, though passersby on the path had detoured primly, alarmed by their incomprehensible gestures.

Poe and Baudelaire looked at each other.

"Eugène Sue is expecting us," said Baudelaire.

"Moreover," said Poe, "I see a gardien approaching."

Raising their hats to the gaping spectators, they resumed their walk with some alacrity toward the great wrought-iron gateway of the Luxembourg Gardens.

"I shall entitle my new opera," Crespigny called after them, *"The Phaeton Boys.* Wave good-bye to them, Gaby," he added, picking up his rat.

Outside the gateway, a fiacre was decanting a passenger. Baudelaire hailed it, but just as they were about to mount into it a hideous scream rang out from behind them. Startled, they turned, looking back.

Crespigny, one hand clasping his nose, with the other was whirling his pet wildly round and round by its tail.

"Good God," said Baudelaire, "he's been bitten by his gravid rat!"

"Infection!" Crespigny screamed, in panic. "Plague! Bubonic! Help! A doctor!"

He let go of his pet, which made a flight of its own, arching high through the air with its ribbon fluttering, and fell with a plop into the bowl of the fountain.

"Baudelaire! Duprez! Help, help!" screeched the composer, both hands clapped to his nose. "Get me to a doctor!"

Poe and Baudelaire looked at each other.

"Serve him right," said Baudelaire, and ducked into the cab.

"*Infirmerie des Indigents,*" Poe instructed the cabman, and joined Baudelaire in the cab.

Through the clip-clop of the horse's hoofs and the jingle of the harness bells, scream after scream followed them as the cab bowled away from the Luxembourg Gardens.

Twelve

It did not occur to Poe or to Baudelaire, as the screams of the hysterical composer ceased to be audible, that few things could be more venomous than the spite of the epicene and that they might have done better not to have abandoned Crespigny but to have taken him to have his nose cauterized.

Nevertheless, with that mercurial alternation of euphoria and manic depression peculiar to the artistic temperament, a somber mood fell upon the strange companions after their flight of airy fancy in the Luxembourg Gardens.

The fiacre was twisting and turning through the maze of narrow streets and noisome alleys in the vicinity of the Rue Tournefort. Night was closing in. Gas lighting had not yet reached this district. Candles guttered and oil glims flickered dimly in kennels where huddled shadows argued and bargained over frugal transactions involving half kilos of flour, a cup of olive oil, a handful of bones, a jug of sour wine, a dish of tripes, a few sticks of charcoal.

Poverty, thought Poe (who knew its pinch so well), preparing to dine.

It was in such alleys as these, where now the mist was thickening, that revolution smoldered.

With the fall of night, garbage fell also, from upper windows. Some of it fell into the fiacre, where it landed at the feet of Poe and Baudelaire. They were protected by the hood, but some of the jetsam, both solid and liquid, fell on the cabman in his more exposed position. He knew better than to look upward to give his views on this manna, but merely hunched his shoulders and suggested viciously to his blameless horse some almost impossible things for the householders to do physically to themselves.

"From olfactory evidence," said Baudelaire, picking up from the foot mat with the ferrule of his stick a wad of sodden newspaper, "this object has been used for what the Reverend Rabelais, in a telling chapter, refers to as a *torchecul.*"

He thrust the sodden wad out into the night, where a shawled figure vaguely female, clomping by in wooden sabots, hugging a cabbage and some animal's bloody haunch, screeched at him for his pains and spat in on his trousers.

"Good God!" said Baudelaire, recoiling. "*Cocher,* how much farther?"

"*Pas loin,* m'sieu," snarled the cabman, and, some five minutes later, reined in his horse. "*Voilà—l'Infirmerie des Indigents!*"

"Wait," Baudelaire ordered, and, holding on his silk hat with a pink-gloved hand, ducked out of the cab, followed by Poe in his caped greatcoat and tall beaver hat.

The paupers' hospital loomed grimly all along one side of

the stinking alley. Through barred, unglassed orifices here and there in the façade of the ancient building weak glimmers showed, and from somewhere within a muffled moaning, as of collective human misery, sounded a dreary, undulant note.

"There's Eugène," said Baudelaire.

They joined the author of *The Rival Races,* who was standing, cloaked and silk-hatted, under a candle lanthorn burning over ponderous, iron-studded doors.

"*Enfin, mes amis,*" he said. "Where have you been?"

"America," explained Baudelaire. "Mephisto here has been tempting his credulous Faust with a display of Earth's fairest cities."

"Monsieur Sue," said Poe, "we're much indebted to you for your participation, as an ex-medical man, in our immediate project."

"Your plan, Monsieur Duprez," said Sue, "has a satanic elegance that appeals to me. General Aupick is a pillar of the established clique, which I oppose. If he can be bamboozled to his detriment, so much the better."

"Have no fear," said Poe. "Diddling, properly considered, ranks among the exact sciences."

"As to that," said Sue, "I agree with you, Duprez, that by hook or crook the patrimony of our young friend here must be liberated. Otherwise, as you've said, compound interest on his debts can ruin his life—and the work that's latent in him."

"Thank you—thank you both," Baudelaire said. "By God, it was my lucky night—the night my American dogged my footsteps and strode upon me, an apparition out of the dark." He looked up at the barred window orifices. "Eugène—that intermittent moaning sound?"

"The evensong of the doomed, Charles," said Sue. "For my part, I've wielded saw and scalpel amid the thunder and smoke of broadsides. The things we classicists do for the Greeks!" He smiled wryly. "As for Duprez here, he's no doubt ridden with the United States cavalry in the Red Indian wars on America's western frontier. He's seasoned. But you, Charles, my young exquisite—can *you* face life in the raw?''

"No poet," said Baudelaire, "should shrink from it."

"But its aroma is better filtered," said Sue. "Fold your handkerchiefs and I'll scent them from this vial."

As he shook drops from the vial onto their handkerchiefs, the horse in the shafts of the waiting fiacre stamped with a harness jingle. Through the swelling and waning of the moan from the infirmary sounded faint, lunatic cries.

Footsteps approached.

Out of the night came a tall, awkwardly bulky man wearing a gravy-hued ulster and a moleskin hat with a peak at the front and at the back. The light from the candle lanthorn glimmered on his vealy face. Under one arm he carried a thick volume with a worn leather cover.

"And here," said Sue, "is Monsieur Laboine—with his Ledger of the Dead."

"Apologies for my tardiness, messieurs," said Laboine. "As burial contractor to this charitable establishment, I have constant calls on my time."

"The dead," Poe said sepulchrally, "are always with us."

"But the better class of citizen prefers them kept off the streets," said Laboine.

"You sent me word," said Sue, "that you'd found us a possible subject."

"I strive to please, Monsieur Sue. Yes, yes"—Laboine ran rheumy eyes over Poe as though measuring him for a winding sheet—"the subject bears a resemblance, as specified, to Monsieur Duprez here. *Quite* a resemblance! And, happily, the subject's a terminal case, so fortunate for your requirements. Come, gentlemen, follow me."

He moved to the ponderous, iron-studded doors. Poe, Baudelaire and Sue tied their triangulated handkerchiefs masklike over their mouths and noses.

The contractor, a hand on the massive latch ring of a

wicket door in the right portal, indicated a smaller wicket door set low down, devoid of latch or handle, in the left portal.

"Turnstile door for alms of clothing and food," he said. He turned the latch ring of the larger wicket, the door creaked open. "This way, gentlemen."

They followed him into a cryptlike chamber, stone-floored, its groined roof upheld by pillars and arches. A few candles guttered from iron wall sconces. Crutches were stacked against the pillars. The undulant moaning sounded more loudly, the atmosphere smelled of dankness and decay.

"*Bonsoir,* Reverend Almoner," said Laboine.

An old nun whose waxen face was as worn as that of a dead saint sat at a small table, an iron-bound alms box open before her, a few coins on the table, on which a single candle burned. Spiked on other candelabra on the table were candle stubs of various lengths, unlighted.

"*Bonsoir,* Monsieur Laboine." Her eyes, darkly alive in the frame of her wimple, looked at the contractor and his masked companions. "You come untimely."

"Business is business." Laboine took up one of the unlighted candelabra. "With permission?" he said, and dipped the wicks of the three candle stubs spiked on the candelabrum to the flame of the candle that burned.

Silent as ghosts, nuns in rough habits of white came and went through the pillared archways, to the dull moan of the damned.

Baudelaire and Sue each laid a gold louis on the table before the almoner, and she folded her knotted fingers over the crucifix of her rosary, bowing her head. But Poe gave nothing, being a pauper come among his kind.

"This way," said Laboine.

They followed the flare of his guttering candles through damp stone corridors, the moaning growing louder. They descended worn stone steps, and an imbecile wail soared shuddering through the moan.

"Oh, my God," Baudelaire breathed, "what a hell hole!"

"You were warned," said Sue.

"Goya," said Poe, epicure of disaster.

"Follow me," said Laboine.

Single file, they picked their way behind him over the flagstones where shadows huddled shapeless on scanty straw. Here and there a dim form heaved up to watch the passage of strangers.

Fire glowed sullenly red from a brazier. A nun tossed a handful of herbs on the smolder, and the herbs flared up briefly, lighting a circle of eyes that stared blankly from matted hair and wrecked faces. The quick flare died, releasing a drift of purifying smoke, to a growing seethe of whispering voices.

"There," said Laboine, "over there in the corner—there's our man."

Under a wall niche where a candle burned before an image of the Virgin, a man lay on a stained palliasse on the floor, and a nun knelt beside him, squeezing water from a rag into a bowl.

Following Laboine, Baudelaire saw blind hands groping. Skeletal, they found his cloak and clutched it, and he looked down, appalled, into a mask of weeping scabs from which eyeballs sightless and colorless rolled up at him.

"*Ayez pitié de moi; mon Dieu, pitié!*"

Laboine turned, striking aside the clinging hands. "*Laissez le monsieur!*"

"*Au secours,*" the hunched form moaned, sinking back. "*Au secours—mon Dieu, mon Dieu—*"

From deeper in the shadows a voice screamed, "*C'est Laboine! C'est l'entrepreneur!*"

The sibilance of whispers swelled through the ward like a buzzing of disturbed hornets, as the intruders reached the corner where lay the man they sought.

Laboine said, "How fares it with him now, Sister Monique?"

The kneeling nun looked up, and she was young, with a calm beauty that the spirit in her held inviolate against all ugliness of life and pain of death.

"As you see," she said, "he sleeps. Pray leave him be."

"Gentlemen, come closer," said the contractor. "Look well."

"What ails him?" Baudelaire murmured through his masking handkerchief.

"Absinthe," said Sue. "It's eaten his liver."

"Just so, a nameless profligate," said Laboine, "self-destroyed. I've many such here in my ledger. Some go to the Val-de-Grâce medical school for pleasantries by the students. Some I bury forthwith, being already half-rotten, and record them by a number for the Hôtel de Ville—'Identity Unknown.'"

"God will know him," said Sister Monique, tranquil in faith.

Laboine said, "Note the resemblance, gentlemen."

The man dying here anonymously looked to be in his middle thirties, his face of a gray pallor, the cheeks sunken, the eyes closed, the dark beard silky and not long grown.

"It's true, Henri," Baudelaire whispered. "The forehead especially. There *is* a resemblance to you."

"Already evident, is it not?" said Laboine, with satisfaction. "But wait till I can get at him, titivate him a little, shave the beard—leave only the moustache, just like monsieur's."

As he glanced at Poe, Laboine's candles, carelessly held, spilled hot wax onto the dying man's left cheek.

"Have a care," said Sister Monique. "Ah, *quelle horreur!* You've scalded him!"

"What odds?" said the contractor. "His calendar's but a leaf or two to run, if that."

"For shame, Monsieur Laboine," said Sister Monique. "Look what you've done."

A blemish burned angrily red on the nameless man's cheek, and he stirred a little, his eyelids twitching.

"He's felt that burn," Sue murmured.

Poe gnawed his moustache, under his masking handkerchief. Presentiment haunted him. In the dying man's physical likeness to himself, and in the alcoholic addiction that had brought the profligate prematurely to this ending, Poe saw the all too likely terminus of his own checkered road through life.

Israfel, he thought, poor, weak, wandering fool. . . .

"Faceless?" murmured the dying man. His eyes glimmered, dazzled by the candleshine as he seemed to become aware of the circle of unknown forms looming huge, with masked faces, over him. His voice was a whisper, barely audible from cracked, fever-dry lips. "Faceless men—"

"Hush," Sister Monique said gently. She bathed his forehead, clustered about by thinning damp curls. "Have no fear."

But fear was growing in him, his eyes opened wider, he drew in a shuddering breath.

"Go, Monsieur Laboine," Sister Monique said. "Go—and take your ghouls with you. For pity's sake, *go,* messieurs. Leave him in peace."

Ashamed, they moved away.

Out of the shadows, stirrings and whispers, a voice shrieked, "*Allez-vous en,* Laboine!"

There was scuffling in the shadows. Figures humped and crawled on all fours over the scattered straw, crying out.

"*Trop tôt! Trop tôt, Laboine! Allez-vous en!*"

A crutch struck the candelabrum from the contractor's hand, and the voices soared in a crescendo of screamed abuse.

"*A bas, l'entrepreneur! Les vers! Mangez-vous les vous-même!*"

The visitors beat an ignominious retreat up the stone stairs.

Sounds of the tumult they had left behind followed them along the corridors and under the arches, and still was audible when they reached the outer chamber where the almoner sat at her table.

She looked at them, and motioned toward the ponderous street doors. Inset low down in one of them, the diminutive turnstile door, which on this side had affixed to it a shallow oaken box, was beginning slowly, stealthily to revolve.

The box was gone.

After a moment, again the turnstile door began to revolve. The oaken box reappeared, now with the gift of a bundle of rags in it.

From the rags came a faint cry—the whimper of a creature newborn.

"The door without wedlock," said Laboine, with a vealy grin.

"Who enters?" said Sue grimly. "A Beethoven? Or an Attila? Rich man, poor man, beggar man, thief?"

"God bless you for your alms," the almoner said quietly.

Baudelaire, tearing off his masking handkerchief, strode to the great doors and, turning the ponderous ring latch, stepped out into the night.

The others joined him. He stood taking great gulps of the night mist.

"Blessed be the Holy Orders, *n'est-ce pas?*" said Laboine, as he drew shut the wicket door. "Once there was a Jesuit who prayed to God for a sign that the Jesuits were the favorite among His Orders. A missive fell from heaven, stating that, of all His Orders, none was a favorite, but all were equally beloved. The missive was signed: 'God, S.J.' Ha-ha-ha, it is droll, is it not?"

"Shut—your—mouth!" Baudelaire said, and he turned abruptly and ducked into the fiacre.

Taken aback, the contractor said, "What ails monsieur there?"

"He's still young enough to weep," Poe said harshly, "for us all."

"She was only a dirty whore," the cabman called reassuringly from his box. "I saw her. She had fox-red hair and slunk like a vixen."

"So, then, Monsieur Laboine," Sue said, "you'll keep me informed?"

"*Bien sûr,* Monsieur Sue. It won't be long now."

"Where to?" asked the cabman.

"To gaslights, wine, and the sound of music," Sue said. "Take us to the Bal d'Ossian."

He ducked into the cab, followed by Poe.

The cabman slapped his reins on the horse's back. "K'ck, k'ck!" Hoofs clopped, harness jingled, the fiacre moved off.

Laboine stood listening to the sound of it receding. He shrugged.

"*Le beau monde*," he said.

He walked away into the dark with his ledger under his arm.

The candle guttered, burning low in the lanthorn above the portals with the turnstile door.

Thirteen

"Not one centime!" said General Aupick emphatically, as he dissected a roast partridge. "You will make *no* advances to Charles, Ancelle. Strict adherence to the quarterly interest payments on what remains of his capital, now soundly invested in the *rentes*, and not one sou more. *That* is the policy you will follow. Is that understood?"

"Certainly, General. Your instructions are always couched in terms of the most helpful clarity—most helpful." Over the napkin tucked into the collar which winged up about his ears, Monsieur Ancelle was flushed with food, wine and embarrassment. "It was just that, on the occasion under advisement, I was—somewhat awkwardly placed, as Monsieur Baudelaire had someone with him. Had he been alone, I should have taken a different stance—*mais naturellement*—immovable, I do assure you, and I should have spoken my mind to him in no uncertain terms.''

Caroline, elegant as always, beautiful in the light winking from the crystals of the chandelier above the oval dining table, had a question to ask.

"Monsieur Ancelle," she said, at her most alluring, "*who* was with Charles? Was it perhaps—a *black* girl?''

"Caroline," Aupick said, drawing his grizzled brows together over the martial beak of his nose, "what do *you* know of this—this black girl?''

"Why, my dear," said Caroline, "you mentioned her yourself. It was the last time Charles visited us—on the night of our ball for the Polish cause, do you not recall?''

"I may possibly have made some passing remark. However, you know no more than that?''

"How could I?" said Caroline lightly. "Monsieur Ancelle, a *soupçon* of butter sauce on your asparagus?''

"*Volontier*," said Monsieur Ancelle, holding out his plate.

General Aupick was not entirely satisfied. He consumed a forkful of partridge, patted his moustache with his napkin. "Caroline, you remember, I trust, my expressed wishes in the matter of visits by you to your son's apartment?''

"I hope I always respect your wishes, dear.''

"So you were, then, elsewhere than in the vicinity of the Hôtel Lauzun, Ile Saint-Louis, for several hours yesterday afternoon?''

"I was at a matinée at the Théâtre du Pantheon in the company of Colonel Yvonnec's wife.''

"And what was the particular attraction of the Théâtre du Panthéon?''

"Most disappointing, I'm afraid—just acrobats and fire-eaters and poodles that walked on their hind legs wearing sailor suits. Monsieur Ancelle, don't you think that kind of performance is rather unnatural?''

"I've never kept dogs, madame—or indeed cats. I once purchased a canary in the Bird Market near the Grands Augustins. I was attracted by the cage, which was in the form of a pagoda. The bird died, but I still have the pagoda."

"Then you mustn't be discouraged," said Caroline. "We must get him a bird, mustn't we, General? I think he feels it, not having a bird. Meantime, Monsieur Ancelle, you were going to tell us about Charles's black girl?"

"I? No, no, madame! In fact," said Monsieur Ancelle, "it was not a—uh—woman of any—any particular pigmentation who accompanied Monsieur Charles to my *étude* the other day. It was his American."

"*His* American?" said General Aupick. "What do you mean by that?"

"Yes," said Caroline, refilling the lawyer's wineglass, "do tell us, Monsieur Ancelle!"

"Well now, you may perhaps recollect, General, an individual who presented himself at your door on the night of your Polish function—"

"That mercenary?" said Aupick, incredulous. "That grotesque adventurer who dares to claim he was at West Point Military Academy and has the effrontery to swagger about the streets in its uniform's greatcoat?"

"The same," admitted the lawyer, cowering a little.

General Aupick laid down his knife and fork. "This is incredible! You're telling me that that obnoxious upstart took it upon himself to drag my stepson to your door and incite him to apply for *money?*"

"Monsieur Charles, if I may say so," stammered the lawyer, "scarcely needed incitement, General. In fact, I must admit the Yankee didn't open his mouth."

"Then what *did* he do?" Caroline asked.

"He—he stood at Charles's side," said Monsieur Ancelle.

"Just stood?" asked Caroline, puzzled.

"He stood and looked at me," said the lawyer. "Monsieur Charles did the talking—presenting his case with, if I may so, his usual plausibility. But the American just stood eying me. He—he has strange eyes."

"Strange?" said General Aupick. "Are you suggesting, Ancelle, that he stood there exerting some psychic influence on you to give Charles money?"

"Well—I wouldn't say that, exactly—"

"But you did give Charles an advance?"

"Well—yes. I—uh—"

"Against my express instructions," said General Aupick, "you advanced Charles money?"

"Very little, General," pleaded Ancelle; "a mere pittance to, in the term so readily used by him, 'tide' him over. You see—"

"Caroline," said General Aupick, "how has this come about? How did your son fall into this—this charlatan's clutches?"

"My dear," said Caroline, "how does Charles come to meet any of his more undesirable companions?"

"As his mother, you should make it your business to know these things."

"And how do you suggest I do that," said Caroline, with spirit, "when you forbid me to see for myself what goes on in his apartment?"

General Aupick took up his knife and fork. "A stepfather," he said bitterly, "no matter what goodwill he may display, what thought he may devote, what kindness he may lavish, what anxiety he may endure, what sleepless nights—"

His voice was beginning to rise to a resounding note of grievance, but just then a knock, barely audible, came from the door, the glass knob turned, and the door opened wide enough to disclose the face of Jean, the flunkey, wincing with apprehension.

"Well?" Aupick demanded. "What is it?"

The flunkey crept in, proffering to General Aupick a silver salver on which lay two visiting cards.

" 'Monsieur Eugène Sue'?" said the General. "And 'Monsieur Théophile Dondey, Licentiate in Profane Letters'? What the devil's this? Did you not tell these people I am dining?"

"Yes, my General, but the elder gentleman said the matter was one of—of grave import, my General."

"To them, possibly, but not to me, whatever it is. Show them into my bureau. They can wait."

The flunkey backed out, leaving General Aupick frowning at the cards. "Sue? Dondey?" He tossed the cards onto the table, took up his cutlery. "They're nobody *I* ever heard of."

"Oh, but, dear," said Caroline, "you must surely have heard of Eugène Sue, the *feuilletoniste?* His newspaper serial is the talk of Paris. It's most exciting."

"Caroline!" Aupick, shocked, stabbed his partridge to the heart. "You mean to tell me that you read *newspaper* serials—sensational twaddle fit only for half-lettered shaven-pated conscripts idling in barrack rooms, seducing and belousing each other?"

"Your nights are less sleepless than you seem to think, dear," said Caroline, sweetly. "I have to do *something* when the sounds you make while slumbering at my side keep me awake."

"Good God!" said the general. He frowned at the visiting cards. "Journalists, are they? H'm! There may have been some leak from our deliberations at the War Ministry. I'd better warn these scribblers at once that if they publish anything whatsoever in their lying sheets I'll have them arrested immediately for the purpose of extorting their sources."

He threw down his napkin, pushed back his chair.

"Caroline, if you'll excuse me? I'll return to you for pudding."

As the door closed on her husband's ramrod back, Caroline fluttered her pretty eyelashes at the lawyer.

"Do *you* think I'll be a nice pudding, Monsieur Ancelle?"

"Pardon?"

"For a general," said Caroline, "to gobble all up?"

His fork suspended, Monsieur Ancelle glanced about him as though seeking elucidation from the ambience.

"The fault is undoubtedly mine," he stammered, "due to a want of acumen, but I'm not sure I follow the purport—"

"Never mind," said Caroline kindly. "Talking of birds, Monsieur Ancelle—as we were, you may remember—a little bird told me that a ballet dancer from Timbuctoo or some such place was appearing at the Théâtre du Panthéon. Unfortunately, when I went there, the bill had changed. Monsieur Ancelle, can you tell me if that equatorial danseuse is by any chance Charles's black inamorata?"

"Madame, I know nothing whatever about Monsieur Charles's black inamorata—should such there be."

"Come now," urged Caroline, "regard it as a privileged communication. After all, I'm Charles's mother, remember." She patted the lawyer's hand coaxingly. "You can be quite open with me."

"I assure you, madame, I am as open as the day. I am entirely in the dark."

"So that's what she remains," said Caroline, disappointed, "a sphinx in sable—or should I say minx? Oh, well! Come, then, Monsieur Ancelle, now that we are cozy together, tell me instead, quite confidentially, *all* you know about Charles's American."

As it happened, Baudelaire's American, and not a high-policy leak from the Invalides, was the topic of the somewhat strained conference in General Aupick's *bureau.*

"I see," the general said grimly, standing rigidly behind his desk, with his back to the portrait of his bovine monarch. "I see. Very well, Monsieur Dondey."

Thoughtfully, Aupick revised the positions of a gun carriage and a battering ram in the model siege train that toiled in operational march across the red-leather terrain of his desktop, then took a cheroot from the silver box on the desk.

He did not offer the box to his callers. Still cloaked, their hats in their hands, they remained standing as Aupick puffed his cheroot alight over the wall gas globe.

"And you, Monsieur Sue," he said, "what is *your* interest in this matter?"

"Monsieur Dondey here is young, General Aupick—inexperienced in such affairs," said Eugène Sue. "Having undertaken to act for Monsieur Duprez, he therefore sought my guidance."

"Monsieur Sue has seen action—in the naval service." O'Neddy's eyes, magnified by the thick lenses of his glasses, blinked sternly at the general. "He is also a qualified physician and surgeon and has consented to act as such in this matter, should it go further."

"It will go just as far as I think necessary, Monsieur Dondey." Aupick strode to the door, threw it open, and shouted across the foyer, "Ancelle!"

Leaving the door open, he returned to his position behind the rampart of his desk.

"Monsieur Ancelle is my man of law," he said. "He happens to be dining with me."

"Our incursion upon your repast," said Sue, "is regrettable."

Ancelle entered in haste, plucking his napkin from his collar.

"You called, General?"

"Ancelle, we have a coincidence here," said General Aupick. "A few minutes ago we were discussing at table an American adventurer and jumped-up military poseur—"

"General Aupick," O'Neddy said stiffly, "you compound your offense!"

"—who stalked out of this house," Aupick continued, undeterred, "on the night of our Polish function, with a bluster of histrionic wrath. You recall that performance?"

The lawyer nodded nervously, dabbing at his mouth with his napkin.

"He chose to consider, on that occasion," Aupick continued, "that I'd cast doubt on his preposterous claim to a West Point background, and aspersions on his health—obviously undermined by intemperance."

"I am sure," said the lawyer apprehensively, "I am fully persuaded that any remarks which may have been exchanged, *en passant*, in the course of general conversation, were assuredly —um—in the legal sense, without prejudice."

"I *now* gather," said General Aupick, "from these two gentlemen, that he claims I've subsequently repeated these alleged 'slanders' in public."

"Oh, no!" said the lawyer, alarmed. "That, no! Unthinkable, gentlemen!"

"My principal," said O'Neddy, his magnified eyes relentless, "demands a written retraction and apology from General Aupick—or equivalent satisfaction."

General Aupick blew out a contemptuous cloud of cheroot smoke.

"In other circumstances, Ancelle," he said, "I might deal differently with this American's impudence. However, in view of what I've heard from various sources—including yourself, this very evening, at my own table—it seems that this fellow Duprez is exerting a sinister influence on my stepson, Charles Baudelaire. For the sake, therefore, of my wife's peace of mind, I welcome this opportunity to put an end to that interloper's mischief, once and for all."

"General—General," the lawyer stammered, "possibly some—some judicial composition—"

"This is not a matter for writs, nor will chastisement with a horsewhip meet the case," General Aupick said grimly. "This is a terminal matter. Be so good as to arrange the details with these—*literary* gentlemen.''

He strode to the door.

''General,'' the lawyer begged, flustered, in panic, ''a brother officer could perhaps more ably—''

General Aupick turned, his eyes cold.

''You are this family's lawyer, Ancelle, and this is a family matter. Pistols, of course. The usual place in the Bois de Boulogne will serve the purpose, and Saturday at dawn will not unduly inconvenience my more important engagements.''

He walked out, slamming the door. And from the open mouth of Monsieur Ancelle, whose partridge was fluttering within him from emotional stress, burst a despairing eructation. His collar points rose about his ears as he clapped his napkin to his lips and turned his horrified eyes on Sue and O'Neddy.

Waiting in a cab at the corner of the Rue Bourbon, Poe and Baudelaire saw light emerge from Number forty-four as the door opened for the egress of Sue and O'Neddy. The door closed behind them, and they walked quickly along the dark street and ducked into the four-wheeler, taking the turndown seats.

''Café Momus, Rue des Prêtres,'' Baudelaire put his head out of the window to tell the cabman. Drawing in his head, he said anxiously, ''Well?''

''Clockwork, Charles,'' said Sue. ''Duprez's plan goes like clockwork.''

''The secret,'' said Poe, ''lies in the precise calculation of juxtapositions.''

The technique, he could not help thinking, was interestingly akin to that of ''The Gold Bug.'' But he kept the thought to himself.

O'Neddy said, excited, ''The lawyer was there, right enough!''

''Thursday,'' said Baudelaire.

''Just so,'' said Poe.

"He's to second General Aupick," said O'Neddy, "with Sue here officiating as surgeon and referee."

"The bait properly placed," said Poe, nodding, "and predictably taken."

"It's to be at the Bois de Boulogne," said Eugène Sue. "Day after tomorrow—at dawn."

"So!" said Poe. "With the aid of your eyeglasses, O'Neddy, the trap is now set. Charles, as the spring snaps, you'll find you hold General Aupick, Ambassador Presumptive to Madrid or the Sublime Porte, helpless in the hollow of your hand."

"My American," said Baudelaire. "My American!"

Fourteen

On the following morning, Friday, when the sun heaved its aureole above the rim of the horizon, the sudden glow was witnessed by a man in ragged raiment and a red stocking cap who was perched high up in the fork of a tall tree.

Rolling away on all sides of his airy perch lay a wide expanse of heathland, about a day's hard ride south of Paris, and the eye of the man up the tree, being the only eye he had, quested the wilderness with an attentiveness all the more acute.

Dew sparkled on the heathery tops of the undulations, dotted with wind-stunted firs and scarred by gravel pits, but daybreak mist still lingered in the hollows. White clouds billowed, with matronly stateliness, high in the vast sky already growing blue. Except for the vanes of a windmill, idly gesticulant in silhouette on a remote eminence, no human habitation or sign of life met the solitary eye of the watcher up the tree.

His vigilant surveillance was concentrated mostly on the white ribbon of road which reached away over the mauve heath toward the southern horizon. And it was there, on the farthest visible point of the highway, that he discerned, after a while, a moving dot.

Even as he saw it, the dot vanished into a hollow. He watched intently.

The dot reappeared, grown slightly larger—and suddenly the man up the tree, which was a horse chestnut, focused his eye directly downward through the jigsaw of branches on which sticky buds were begining to swell. He whistled piercingly through decayed front teeth.

The tree in which he was perched reared its height from a coppice of birches, the silver of their boughs faintly stippled with the tender livery of spring. The coppice extended to either side of a dip in the road, where a stream flowed brandy-brown through a culvert.

Below the arborealist on his high perch, two saddled horses were tethered, and on the bank of the stream a stout man and an old woman lay spread-eagled, face down.

The stout man was sucking up water from the stream, but the old woman, inactive, was merely spread-eagled. Everything about her was old, from the worn-out button boots protruding from beneath the ragged hems of her skirts and petticoats, to the tangle of gray hair that straggled meekly from under her jet-beaded bonnet.

Not only was she old, but also tired, or even dead, for she made no response to the warning whistle of the one-eyed tree-climber.

The stout man, however, reared to his feet and, wiping water from his mouth and nose with his sleeve, upturned a black-stubbled, brutal face and shouted, *"Oui?"*

The man aloft, who was long, lean and of a shambling build, had refocused his eye on the far reaches of the road, where the moving object, growing rapidly larger, was now identifiable as a team of six horses at a rapid canter, hauling a coach of the long-distance mail type.

"Oui!" yelled the one-eyed man, and at once, with the elastic alacrity of an agile gibbon, came swiftly from branch to branch down the tree.

He leaped to the ground, and the two men—the lean one in the red stocking cap and the stout one whose stocking cap was green—laid hold on the old woman. Receiving no protest from her, the two men loped, carrying her face down by her boots and the old stays bursting through the hooks and eyes of her dress, to the edge of the road.

Here they paused to peer furtively to their left along the road where it meandered away northward across the heath, while the old woman's head in its bombazine bonnet nodded limply downward.

Seeing no moving object on the road to the north, the men loped out from the shelter of the coppice, laid the old woman face down in the middle of the road, where the culvert made a slight hump, and loped back, bent double, into the trees.

Untethering the two horses, the men mounted them, then pulled their stocking caps completely down over their faces. The stout man's green stocking cap had two eyeholes in the knitting. Heeling his horse's flanks, he rode across the road without so much as a glance through his eyeholes at the old woman spread-eagled tiredly on the culvert's hump. Gaining the other side of the road, he took station among the trees there and searched out a pistol from one of the many rents and tears noticeable in his attire.

The lean man, astride his horse, stayed where he was, he also with a pistol in his hand. His red stocking cap, despite his monocular vision, nevertheless was provided with twin eyeholes, one to look out through, the other no doubt designed to falsify subsequent depositions by witnesses of the act about to be perpetrated.

For a while, as the men, one each side of the road, lurked thus in ambush, there was no sound but the chuckle of the stream as it tumbled in freshet under the culvert. Then, from the south, a faint thudding became audible, grew rapidly louder, and proclaimed itself as proceeding from the hoofs of a team of horses approaching at a fast canter.

Rattling and creaking mingled with the thud of hoofs and the grind of iron-shod wheels—and suddenly, huge against the sky, the six horses hauling the Paris Mail swept into view, with tossing manes and flared nostrils, over the brow of the hollow.

The ambushers cocked their pistols.

Down the slope thundered the six-in-hand with the coach jolting and rattling after them. Perched high on the box beside the coachman, and holding on tightly to the foot-rest rail, was a hatless girl with fair hair streaming exuberantly in the wind.

A certain master plotster, asleep in a curtained recess in a house in the Place Dauphine, a day's ride distant, might have recognized the girl on the box, from a miniature in his possession. But she had no place in his dreams, nor could he know that the events about to occur on a section of the *route nationale* might materially affect, for better or for worse, his maturely considered stratagems.

Kate Casteign and the coachman spotted simultaneously the old woman in the middle of the road, helplessly spread-eagled on the slight hump of the culvert.

"Stop!" Kate screamed. *"Stop!"*

She expected the coachman to haul back on his reins, bringing the horses rearing to a standstill. But no, the coachman was a seasoned old *routier,* wary of coppices in hollows. His quick eyes searched the birches to either side of the culvert, and he saw a movement among them, the glint of a snaffle ring and a glimpse of red wool amid the pristine green.

At once, instead of reining in his horses, he stood up on the footboard and poured his whip into them.

"Alerte!" he roared to the postilion, perched behind in his high dickey seat.

The horses tore at a full gallop down the slope. Kate covered her eyes with one hand, clinging to the jolting rail with the other, as the plunging hoofs of the horses hammered down on the old woman and the wheels of the coach heaved heavily over her and the hump of the culvert.

Taking her hand from her face, Kate looked back, shuddering, her gray eyes wide with horror.

Extensively mashed, the old woman was clearly done for. The large swede of her head, divested alike of wig and bonnet, was rolling to the side of the road. The turnips of her bosom and buttocks were crushed to mere vegetable blotches. Her old boots had been hurled aside and lay in amputated isolation on the hump of the culvert. Her stays had burst asunder from the now shattered broom handle which had served her, scarecrow-wise, for a spine.

But even as Kate saw these pathetic remains of an old woman, two furious horsemen rode out from the coppice, one from the left of the road, one from the right. Masked by stocking caps of green and red wool respectively, the horsemen brandished pistols as they frantically jockeyed their mounts to a gallop in pursuit of the coach.

"Highwaymen!" Kate screamed to the coachman, as she grasped both the situation and the rocking box rail.

The coachman, standing, swaying like a charioteer, lashed his whip into his tearaway horses.

"Hue, cocotte!"

Kate twisted her neck to look back. The postilion, too, was twisted around in his dickey seat, trying to bring his musket to bear on the pursuing horsemen.

Kate saw a wink òf flame spurt from the pistol of the horseman in the green stocking cap. Something cracked wickedly near her left ear.

"A bullet!" she screamed to the coachman. "We're being

shot at!'' Exalted, she thought, Oh, if only Henry could see me now!

How often had she dreamed that she might one day figure in the role of an authentic heroine! No matter how near death, this was living.

The postilion's musket went off. The report was frightful, but the pursuers seemed undeterred by it.

"They're gaining!" Kate cried to the coachman.

He lashed away at his horses. His language was an education in itself, but it was lost on Kate, who had learned her French from a governess.

"They're level with us!" she screamed to the coachman, as the pursuers came racing up, one on either side of the coach.

At this crucial moment, Lady Casteign, roused from a light drowse by suddenly excessive jolting and the detonations of musketry in her vicinity, thrust her head out of the window to see what was going on.

Her hat, together with her veil and her hind hairpiece, flew off, but her eyes encountered a galloping horseman in an open-work costume of wind-flapping tatters and a red stocking-cap mask racing madly alongside the coach, brandishing a pistol.

Grasping the situation in one outraged glance, she groped behind her for the first missile to come to hand, which happened to be her tea basket. Swinging it by its handle, she aimed a blow with it at the horseman. It struck him heavily on his pistol elbow and burst open, releasing a deluge of cups, saucers, spoons, teapot, tea caddy, strainer, and biscuit barrel painted with views of Balmoral Castle.

The masked rider shot her a venomous glance through one of his two eyeholes as his horse, galvanized by a crash of tea things under his tail, lunged forward with a convulsion that carried the man from Lady Casteign's view.

But not from Kate's, up on the heaving box. She saw both riders galloping to reach the heads of the lead horses with the obvious intention of seizing the reins and forcing the team to a standstill. Almost in the same instant, she saw something else—jogging metal objects, far along the road ahead. They caught the low-slanting beams of the early sun with a multiplicity—momentarily puzzling to Kate—of winking, brassy sparkles.

A certain master plotster, asleep in Paris, had he known what was happening on the *route nationale,* and seen those brassy sparkles, might have groaned in his slumbers, recognizing a cruel intervention of fate in his stratagems, but he was dreaming of other things.

As it was, it was Kate who identified the dancing sparkles.

Pointing at them, she screamed at the coachman, "Helmets?"

The coachman saw them, then.

"Soldiers!" he roared, and poured his whip with renewed energy into his team.

The highwaymen also, just then, spotted the sparkle of helmets, and they reined in their mounts so harshly that they reared and, pulled into a violent turn, departed with extreme urgency in the opposite direction.

"Dragoons!" roared the coachman—and, gesticulating with his whip at the oncoming cavalry squadron, pointed out with the whip the rapidly retreating marauders.

Seeming instantly to appreciate the problem, the officer in the lead immediately unsheathed his saber. The blade flashed like white lightning as he waved his squadron into the charge and came on fast with his saber rigidly leveled at arm's length before him in a style that might, had he been able to see it and had the circumstances been different, have met with the professional approval of a master plotster, sometime of West Point.

"Dragoons of Courbevoie!" roared the coachman, as the straining coach horses and the glittering cavalry with drawn sabers converged upon each other at a headlong gallop.

"Way!" shouted the coachman, in warning. "Make way!"

The squadron opened with drilled precision.

"Way for the Paris Mail!" roared the coachman, as the coach thundered through the squadron.

Clinging to the rail, Kate twisted her neck to look back. The postilion was trying to steady his coaching horn to his lips. Far along the road Lady Casteign's refreshment impedimenta lay scattered like the trail for a tea chase.

The foiled marauders, abandoning the road, were now, red stocking cap and green, riding for their lives—or their liberty from the prison hulks—across the open heath. After them, at full gallop, spurred the young officer with extended saber, the helmets of his tall dragoons, glinting and tossing their horsehair plumes, behind him.

Lady Casteign's head protruded from the coach window. Her neck twisted as she looked up at the box.

"Kate!" she screeched. "Tell the coachman to stop! My tea things!"

"Oh, Mother!" cried Kate. Still in her ears sounded that exhilarating whipcrack of a passing bullet. "Tea things!" she cried, exalted. *"When I might never have lived to see Henry again!"*

She looked out over the heath, just in time to catch a glimpse of the pursued and the pursuers as they passed from view over a ridge in the approximate direction of the remote windmill.

The postilion, unable to blow a blast from his horn without knocking his teeth out because of the jolting of the coach, felt obliged in some way to express his sense of triumph. He began, in a fine baritone voice, to sing the *Marseillaise*. The coachman joined in with a fruity bass. Kate, in her exaltation, could not resist contributing her tuneful soprano.

"Marchons—marchons—"

The Paris Mail tore on, unchecked, toward the ever-nearing capital.

In his bead-curtained recess adjoining Jeanne Duval's salon in the house in the Place Dauphine, the master plotster awoke with a start. He lay gazing up at the samovar dimly perceptible on the shelf above his couch in the dim, stuffy little cubbyhole.

Poe felt strangely uneasy.

Fifteen

His uneasiness persisted as, in the exotic little sponge-bath closet of Jeanne Duval's fifth-floor love nest, he shaved with the razor forsaken by Baudelaire in favor of the cultivation of his fashionable beard, and trimmed his moustache with Jeanne's nail scissors, inconveniently curved.

Studying his dark-circled eyes reflected in the looking-glass daylit from the small skylight, Poe identified the cause of the uneasiness with which he had awakened.

Would the anticipated demise of the nameless profligate in the *Infirmerie des Indigents* eventuate in time for his mortal clay to play its allotted part in his, Poe's, master plot for the de-sequestration of Baudelaire's depleted patrimony?

There lay the nub of Poe's anxiety.

Toward noon, after Baudelaire himself had gone off to carry out an essential errand appertaining to Poe's plan, and Jeanne's daily domestic had arrived, destroyed Poe's concentration, as domestics will, and duly departed, a messenger jangled the front doorbell of the apartment and, inquiring "Monsieur Henri Duprez?", handed Poe a note.

It was from Eugène Sue and it informed Poe that the nameless profligate had indeed delivered up his soul according to schedule and that his perishable remains were now receiving the necessary titivation from the experienced hands of Monsieur Laboine.

The news relieved Poe's anxiety in one sense, the practical, but left him even more uneasy in another, the spiritual. The craftsman in him, the plot-making faculty in which he took pride, was all too often at odds with the artist in him, so inconveniently emotional.

The dead pauper was a mere puppet in the plan of the craftsman, but the artist in Poe was imaginatively troubled by the late profligate's physical resemblance to himself and by the cause and place of the man's death.

Israfel, Poe thought. Poor, fallen fool—at peace now, surely?

He made an effort to shake off a debilitating sense of identification with his puppet. There were practical matters that required attention.

From the deep pocket of his greatcoat, hanging in his sleeping recess, he took the articles of obvious sentimental value which he had found in Henry Lane Duprez's trunk and scrupled to pawn at the Vigo Monte de Piedad.

Looking at them, he thought, "I'm using another man's name. I'm now about to use yet another man's body. Who—and what—am *I?*"

Putting down the things on Jeanne's coffee table—the gold watch with its distinctive fob, the small box containing the returned engagement ring, the oval miniature of the fair-haired, gray-eyed girl whose name he could not remember—Poe wondered if Duprez was alive or dead. He wondered if this girl in the miniature, wintering in Spain with her mother, ever had received any of the letters which Duprez had said he had written to her. He thought of frail Virginia and her mother, sturdy and uncomplaining Mrs. Clemm, and wondered if the act of oblivion he had committed in taking another man's identity had served its purpose, so that they were safe now in the care of rich, righteous Mr. Allan of Richmond. Would Virginia and Aunt Maria Clemm, Poe wondered, know in their hearts *why* he had left them? Or would they—all the rest of their lives . . .

No! He dared not think about that.

Charcoal smoldered in Jeanne's little censer bowl, with its lid off, on the table with the bamboo pipes and the tweezers in the black-smeared cloisonné saucer.

Fanning the charcoal with his handkerchief, he thought again of the pauper, his other self, being prepared for his role by Eugène Sue and Monsieur Laboine.

"Israfel—" Give him a name, Poe thought, for his last appearance on the world's stage before the contractor's barrow trundled him to the Buttes Chaumont and the *cimetière des indigents*—potter's field. "Israfel—"

Poe picked up Jeanne's lute from the ottoman, moved to the window between its heavy velvet curtains, draped and pelmeted.

The upper windows of the tall old houses opposite, with their shutters and small wrought-iron balconies, glinted in sunshine. To his left Poe glimpsed the equestrian statue of Henri IV on the Pont-Neuf arching the slowly gliding Seine.

Israfel, Poe thought; "A litany for all lost men. . . ." He stroked a note absently from the lute, murmuring, "In Heaven a spirit doth dwell/Whose heart-strings are a lute—"

Under the trees with their first gleams of green, five floors down, there in the tiny Place Dauphine, hucksters and housewives chaffered among stalls, tumbrils and hand-barrows. Life went on.

But Poe stroked the lute gently, murmuring, "None sing so wildly well/As the angel Israfel—"

A bead curtain rattled behind him. He turned.

Jeanne drifted into the salon from her bedroom. Drowsy, in diaphanous negligée through which glimmered the ebony of her dancer's perfect body, her hair unbound, she paused at the sight of Poe, black-clad and pale of face, the lute in his hands, there between the window curtains.

"Good morning, Jeanne," he said. "You look surprised to see me."

"Where's Charles?" Jeanne asked.

"Gone to Neuilly—for converse with Monsieur Ancelle."

"Friday," said Jeanne. "No money, I suppose. How tiresome!" She fell among the cushions on the ottoman. "*Oh,* I'm sleepy!"

"You haven't got up yet."

"Give me a crème de menthe. I have a bad taste in my mouth."

"Haven't we all?" said Poe.

He filled a liqueur glass for her from one of the decanters that stood in a niche of the padded wall. From another niche, the gorilla head leered.

"Where did these come from," Jeanne asked, taking the glass from him, "these things on the table?"

"From a trunk I—parted with at Vigo." Poe picked up the lute again.

"Who's this girl in the miniature?" asked Jeanne, examining it.

"I've forgotten her name," said Poe. He shrugged. "When I look at a woman, I see a skeleton."

"This ring is pretty," said Jeanne. "Can I have it?"

"Willingly, kind hostess, if it were mine to give to you."

"Whose is it, then? This girl's? This nameless lady's?"

"It may fit the finger—the pinky," said Poe, "of some— nameless other—who's gone—yet palely loiters still."

He stroked the lute.

"Sometimes," said Jeanne, with a pout of her beestung lips, "you and Charles amuse me. You're mad together. But alone, Henri, you're too often in a mood."

"I'll sing for my supper," said Poe, and drew his thumb over the lute strings. "If I could dwell/Where Israfel/Now dwells and he where I—" He repeated, desolate, his mind far off, "And *he* where I—"

"Put *down* my lute," said Jeanne. "And tell me—if Charles can get no money from his miser at Neuilly, can't we pawn this watch?"

"If it were mine—gladly. But it's not."

"Even so, wouldn't you do it for Charles? You say you esteem him."

"I love that man," Poe said, with the harshness of resolve, knowing what must be done. "I'll show you!" He tossed the lute onto the ottoman, went to the coffee table. "Jeanne, d'you see this charcoal?"

"I thought our poppy was all gone."

"I lit the charcoal for another purpose—in which you can help me."

"Henri, I'm *sleepy!*"

"Then this will wake you up. It's for Charles, Jeanne."

Poe dropped to his knees on the carpet, so that he was on a level with her. He took the glass from her hand, put the glass on the table, picked up the tweezers from the cloisonné saucer.

"What *is* this?" said Jeanne. "Why are you sweating all of a sudden?"

Poe's pallor was enhanced, there were beads on his prominent forehead thrusting from his thinning curls.

"Fear," he said.

"But you're a soldier."

"Steeled to meet death with a smile," said Poe. "But little wounds hurt." He took her hand with its silver-painted nails and put the tweezers into her pink palm. "Now, Jeanne—pick out from the charcoal bowl a red-hot sliver."

"What game is this?" said Jeanne, becoming interested as she picked up with the tweezers a glowing, faintly crackling sliver of charcoal.

"Playing with fire," said Poe. "It's woman's nature—to burn some man. And so you shall." He smiled a dreadful smile. "Come, then, my pitchfork Fury—brand me!"

"*What?*"

"Here—on the left cheek—where my finger points."

"You're mad!"

Sweating, his teeth clenched, Poe said, "Brand me, Jeanne!"

"You *mean* this?"

"It's for Charles. Brand me!"

Her breathing quickened. Her eyes shone, amber, into his.

"Closer," she whispered. "Closer, Henri—"

"Make haste! Make haste!"

"Closer—*closer*—"

Suddenly, as he braced himself, rigid, and they stared demoniacally into each other's eyes, the sliver glowing red hot was pressed, searing, to his cheek. He gasped. Jeanne let fall the tweezers clattering into the saucer. Her ebon breasts heaved.

"Maniac! Madman!" she panted. "I always knew it. You *made* me! Imbecile American!"

"You enjoyed it—you loved it," said Poe. "Jungle savage!"

"Your face!" She pointed at its painful grimaces. "Your face!"

Poe clapped his handkerchief to it, as Jeanne, staring wildly at him, was shaken by laughter.

The gorilla joined in soundlessly, with bared fangs, from the wall niche.

"Nonsense!" shouted Baudelaire, exasperated, and his stick slammed down on a stack of pink-taped dossiers on Monsieur Ancelle's desk.

Dust rose in clouds, here in the lawyer's Neuilly *étude* lined around with exciting volumes explanatory of Torts and revealing on Testaments.

Ancelle, seated behind his desk, wore that air of dignified affront which was his normal expression when not quailing before his most distinguished client, General Aupick.

"Monsieur Charles," said the advocate, "I have known you since you were a charming little school boy in a black pinafore, and I've watched with sincere grief your development into a—"

"Into a what, Monsieur Ancelle?" said Baudelaire dangerously.

"I hardly like to say, Monsieur Charles. Suffice it that I can vouch, from anxious observation, for the fact that your stepfather, General Aupick, has always treated you with exemplary patience."

"Patience is the weapon used by the righteous to blackmail the ardent!"

"Monsieur Charles," said Ancelle, shaking his head, "you grieve me."

Baudelaire, pink-gloved, silk-hatted, in waistcoat embroidered with tiny *fleur de lis,* his cape purple-lined, his beard impeccably barbered, mastered with an effort the intense irritability which invariably arose in him like a swarm of wasps at the mere sight of the lawyer who sat with such complacent self-satisfaction on his, Charles Baudelaire's, paternal nest egg. But he was not here this morning to quarrel, no matter how grossly provoked, and he forced a smile of disarming reasonableness.

"Monsieur Ancelle, isn't this rather absurd? Let us call a truce to this domineering at each other. I came here today in some disturbance of mind—"

"I can well believe it, Monsieur Charles, and I'm the more sorry to find myself obliged to inform you that not one centime is available to you pending the advent of Quarter Day."

"Money?" said Baudelaire, offended. "Who said anything about money?"

"Your stepfather," replied the lawyer. "General Aupick made his wishes so abundantly clear to me that I fear you've had a wasted journey today, Monsieur Charles. I am, I assure you, utterly resolved. Your undeniable charm is powerless to wheedle one further sou—"

"Money, money, money!" said Baudelaire. "Monsieur Ancelle, I beg you, make an effort to rid yourself occasionally of this bourgeois preoccupation. I've come here to consult you about a much graver matter that's come to my ears. This duel!"

"Oh, Monsieur Charles!" Ancelle's defiance deserted him. "Oh, how unfortunate! What a disaster this duel is!"

"My sole concern, naturally," said Baudelaire, "is for my mother. You well know her devotion to the general—"

"Indeed it becomes her," said Ancelle, touched. "Your dear mother, if I may say so, is profoundly womanly. She worships the ground the general—"

"—will lie under," said Baudelaire, "if he gets killed to-morrow!"

"Impossible!" Ancelle recoiled at the horror of it. "The general is a crack shot!"

"But remember—Duprez was trained at West Point."

"But *was* he? That's just the point at issue."

"This is no time," said Baudelaire coldly, "for playing on words."

"What do you mean? You talk in riddles. All I know is that I pray on my bended knees that the Yankee lied."

"Prayer and bended knees, Monsieur Ancelle, are the last resort of the undone."

"I *am* undone! We are *all* undone! Nothing can halt this bloody business!"

"Its issue can be predetermined." Baudelaire pointed his stick compellingly at the lawyer. "By *you!*"

"Oh, Monsieur Charles, what nonsense is this?"

"Monsieur Ancelle, the responsibility of loading the pistols will fall to Eugène Sue, as referee and surgeon, under the scrutiny of yourself and Théophile Dondey, as seconds."

"Well, unaccustomed as I am to affairs of this kind, and

though I regard them as quite gratuitous flirtings with death when a suit in damages, well argued, would more sensibly serve the purpose of the plaintiff, I have at least some general notion of the accepted procedure, Monsieur Charles.''

"So, then,'' said Baudelaire, ''for my mother's sake, Monsieur Ancelle, I sat up throughout most of last night, exerting my powers of persuasion as a devoted son. Excuse me a moment.''

He went to the door, opened it, spoke through the doorway.

"Will you kindly come in, gentlemen?''

Eugène Sue and O'Neddy walked in. Under his arm Sue carried a box made of polished mahogany.

Sue said coldly, "Good day, Monsieur Ancelle,'' but O'Needy restricted himself to staring accusingly, with eyes greatly magnified by his glasses, at the bewildered jurist.

"Mosieur Sue,'' said Baudelaire, ''will you be so good as to show Monsieur Ancelle the contents of that box?''

"Certainly.''

Placing it on the desk before Ancelle, Sue unlocked the box with a small silver key, threw back the lid.

"Pistols!'' said Ancelle, recoiling.

"And there,'' said Baudelaire, pointing with his stick, ''in those leather loops in the red baize of the lid lining?''

"Cartridges,'' said Ancelle.

"Examine one,'' suggested Eugène Sue, ''more minutely.''

Nervously, Ancelle possessed himself of a cartridge and peered narrowly at it.

"But,'' he said, ''but—surely.''

"Well?'' said Sue, and O'Neddy's eyes enlarged behind his glasses.

"But this,'' said Ancelle, ''this appears . . . but good God!'' he exclaimed.

"*Now* do you understand,'' said Baudelaire, "*Maître* Ancelle?''

The lawyer looked up slowly, with a dawning comprehension, at the implacable faces of the three men of letters.

Sixteen

Neither they nor the brain that manipulated them, that of the fourth man of letters, master plotster, wizard of contrivance, user of aliases, had knowledge of the arrival in Paris, long after dark on that fateful Friday night, of the express mail coach from the south.

Clattering over the *pavé* of the Porte d'Italie into the city, the coach rolled presently to a standstill in the yard of the inn and livery stables which were its official terminal.

"Et voilà!" bawled the coachman. *"Enfin, messieurs les voyageurs!"*

Lackeys bustled out from the inn with lanthorns to unload the luggage, as Goubillon, the student of philosophy, raised

Kate's gloved hand to within an inch of the dewdrop on his nose and expressed the hope that she and her mother would sleep none the worse for the morning's outrageous incident on the highway.

"*He* was no help," said Lady Casteign acidly, as the philosopher departed, sniffing, into the night, carrying his carpetbag. "He cowered down in the coach all through that disgraceful affair—about which, I may add, I intend to lodge an immediate complaint with the British Ambassador, the Prefect of the Seine, the Postmaster-General, and the contracting coach company. I intend to recover the cost of my tea things."

"Oh, Mother, how can you keep harping about your tea things," said Kate, "when here we are, providentially preserved, *in* Paris and perhaps within a stone's throw of my darling Henry at this very moment? Come, we can hire a cab from these stables."

"Cab? We can spend the night at this inn. What do we want a cab for?"

"To go straight to the address Eleanor Gerrard wrote to me from," Kate explained. "Heaven send she's still there, because *she* may know where Henry's to be found."

"Kate, I don't intend to move another inch tonight!"

"Mother, we can't afford to lose a minute. If we find Eleanor and she says Henry's left for the battlefields, we must see at once about getting seats in the next mail coach leaving for Belgium, the Low Countries, Pomerania and Warsaw."

"*Warsaw?*" screamed Lady Casteign.

"There may be a coach leaving at dawn," said Kate. "In any case, Eleanor wrote from an *hôtel* in the Rue des Saints Pères, and I'm sure we'll find more comfortable rooms there than here."

Nobody could have the experience of being under fire without being changed by it, and the adventure on the highway and the memory of that bullet crack so close to her ear had endowed Kate with a new firmness of character. This prevailed over Lady Casteign, who could sense the change in the girl. Accordingly, they drove to the Rue des Saints Pères, where Kate hurried immediately into the *auberge* to inquire for Eleanor, leaving Lady Casteign to pay the cabman and see to the off-loading of the luggage.

"Mademoiselle Gerrard?" the *patronne d'auberge* said to Kate. "Ah, *la charmante Americaine! Mais oui, mademoiselle— par là, voyez-vous, dans le salon!*"

Sure enough, there in the salon, Kate found her friend from North Carolina. She was in the company of a short, stout man with a head like a billiard ball. They were seated in basket chairs under the fronds of a potted palm, Eleanor sipping a *tisane* and the short man, Sir Bartle Mole, a glass of port.

"Eleanor!" cried Kate.

"Kate!" cried Eleanor, putting down her cup.

They fell into each other's arms.

"Where is he?" Kate demanded, breathless.

"Where's who?"

"Henry, of course! Henry Lane Duprez of New Orleans whom you met on the roof of Notre Dame! I'm *engaged* to him!"

"Engaged?" Eleanor looked stunned. "Engaged to that— that—"

"That *what*, Eleanor?"

"Never mind! Well, Kate—this *is* a surprise!"

"Eleanor, where *is* he?" Kate begged. "Has he left for Poland yet? Oh, please don't tell me that!"

"But, honey, how in the world would *I* know where he is? I never dreamed *you* were engaged to that—that—"

"Hah-humph!" said Sir Bartle warningly.

Lady Casteign joined the party. "Eleanor! So you *are* here, you poor headstrong child!" She embraced Eleanor protectively, with an inimical eye on Sir Bartle. "And there, presumably, stands Sir Bartram Pole!"

"Mole, ma'am," said Sir Bartle, with a bow. "The name is Mole—Bartle of the ilk—Squire of Mole Park, near Winchcombe, in Gloucestershire."

Ignoring Sir Bartle's courtly welcome, Lady Casteign said, "Eleanor, I will take a dish of tea, if that can be obtained in this place."

"At your service, ma'am," said Sir Bartle. He clapped his hands, calling, "Patrong—madame voolis pronney du tea—toot sweet!"

"*Oui,* monsieur," called the *patronne.*

"She understood me, Eleanor," said Sir Bartle, not without pride.

But Eleanor, excited about something else, said, "Kate, I've had a thought! The man who *may* know what's become of your—your Mr. Duprez is Colonel Sauvagnac, of the Lafayette Circle. You recall, Sir Bartle? The Colonel promised to do what he could to help Mr. Duprez obtain a military appointment in Poland."

"Death in battle!" Kate exclaimed. "Self-sacrifice! He thinks, poor dear, that suicide is all he has to live for. Eleanor, I beg you, take me to this Colonel immediately."

"Kate," said Lady Casteign, "I have not the remotest intention of stirring from this chair until I have taken a dish of tea."

"Stay here, Lady Casteign," said Eleanor. "Sir Bartle will look after you, and I'll look after Kate."

The girls hurried off. Lady Casteign flipped up the lenses of her lorgnette and examined Sir Bartle, who was standing, from his spats to the crown of his polished head.

"H'm," she said. "Well, sir, what have you to say for yourself?"

"Why, ma'am," said Sir Bartle, somewhat surprised, "I trust you've enjoyed—um—a comfortable journey?"

"Do not beg the issue, sir," said Lady Casteign. "I may tell you that I am personally acquainted with Mr. Randolph Ravenel Gerrard, Eleanor's father. I am sure he will take a grave view of the information that Eleanor is conspicuously compromising herself in the lax moral atmosphere of Paris."

"Compromising herself?"

"With a man," said Lady Casteign, "more than old enough to know what he's doing to the girl—and he, to boot, by his own account, a baronet!"

"A knight, ma'am—an humble knight." Sir Bartle's head was turning slowly from a white billiard ball into a red one. "Are you suggesting, ma'am—"

"You know very well what I am suggesting! Come, sir, am I to doubt the evidence of my own eyes? I see you domiciled here shamelessly under the same roof with that foolish girl. What, do you think I was born yesterday?"

"Ma'am—"

"Your designs upon her are all too transparent, sir. I can only pray that I have mercifully arrived here in time to avert the ultimate—"

"Ma'am! *Ma'am!*" Sir Bartle, scarlet, was approaching apoplexy.

Just in time to save him from it, there was a rush of petticoats into the salon, with a chirrup of excited young voices.

"Oh, Papa! Do look! Eleanor took us to all the best shops and we've been trying on our new dresses! Real Paris dresses, Papa! Do—"

The chirrup of the four rather stockily built young women, in their fine raiment and their varying degrees of rosy homeliness, faltered as Lady Casteign's lorgnette was turned upon them.

"Ma'am," said Sir Bartle, in a voice of thunder, "I, too, am acquainted with Eleanor's father. Finding myself unable to persuade her to leave Paris for a visit to Winchcombe, I felt it my duty to Mr. Gerrard, who was a kind host to me in America, to see to it that she was not left in Paris without chaperonage. I therefore," trumpeted Sir Bartle, taking out his snuffbox, "sent to Winchombe for my four daughters—my English roses, as I call them—Freda, Frances, Felicity, and Flo—"

"Your servant, ma'am," chorused the girls shyly, with the

somewhat rustic bobs which passed for curtseys in the simple but wholesome society circles of Winchombe in Gloucestershire.

"Sir Bartle," said Lady Casteign, in a curiously small voice, as she folded her lorgnette, "I seem to have been misled in my—"

"Grossly so, ma'am," said Sir Bartle, still scarlet. "Grossly so!"

To prevent himself from adding, "It comes from poking your long nose into what's none of your business!" he treated each of his own nostrils, in turn, to a gigantic pinch of snuff.

The resultant explosion, though reverberant, failed to reach from the Rue des Saints Pères to the cab in which Kate and Eleanor were then approaching the Pont du Carrousel, over the Seine which in its dark waters reflected tremulously the lines of gas globes that stretched away on both banks into the night mist.

On arriving at the fine old mansion in the Faubourg Saint-Honoré which housed the headquarters of the Lafayette Circle, the girls were admitted by the octogenarian butler, whose faculties were not so impaired by hard knocks in bygone battles that he failed to recognize Eleanor.

"I will inform Colonel Sauvagnac that you are here, Miss Gerrard."

Leaving the girls in the hall, he hobbled off to the handsome double doors that led to the salon, tapped on them and went in, closing the doors behind him.

"That old, old butler, Kate," said Eleanor, "is an actual survivor of the Marquis de Lafayette's detachment that forded the Schuylkill."

"Oh, how marvelous!" said Kate. "Why did they have to ford it?"

"Why, I guess it was on account of Lord Howe," said Eleanor, "advancing from New York and seizing the bridge."

"We British always seem to be seizing something—or trying to," said Kate, admiring the great battle paintings of British defeats that hung on the walls in the light from the chandeliers.

"But never mind, Eleanor; it's all over now and I shall be American myself when I've saved Henry and married him. What does one have to do to become American?"

"I think you have to memorize the names of the Presidents, Kate."

"I'm not very good at memorizing," Kate admitted. "All those Plantagenet and Tudor kings and their dates get me fearfully muddled."

"Well, there aren't all that many Presidents, so far," said Eleanor. "But, you know, Kate, somehow Mr. Duprez's not quite the kind of man I thought *you* would fall in love with."

"Why ever not?"

"Well—he was behaving kind of oddly among the gargoyles of Notre Dame. There's something about him—how shall I say—"

"Unique?"

"Well, I guess so—unique in a bizarre kind of way."

"Eleanor! *Bizarre?*"

"Ah, Miss Gerrard!" Sauvagnac emerged from the salon, followed by the old butler, who closed the doors and hobbled away. Immaculate in civilian evening dress, the Corsican colonel bowed over Eleanor's hand. "Welcome as always!"

"Kate," said Eleanor, "may I introduce Colonel Sauvagnac, a friend of my father's? This is Miss Kate Casteign, Colonel, just this evening arrived from Italy after an exciting journey."

"Miss Casteign," said Sauvagnac, with a bow.

"Colonel," said Eleanor, "we've come to seek information from you. We're wondering if you could help us trace the whereabouts of Mr. Henry Lane Duprez, of New Orleans. You may remember him?"

"I *well* remember the gentleman you brought here, Miss Gerrard. As a matter of fact"—Sauvagnac gave Eleanor a strange look—"it's a curious chance that you should come here with this inquiry at just this time."

"You have *news* of him, Colonel?" Kate asked eagerly.

"As it happens," Sauvagnac said, "I've had news of him within the past hour—regrettable news, I'm afraid."

"He's reached Poland!" Kate exclaimed, paling. "He's fallen!"

"No, no, nothing of the kind—at least, not to my knowledge," said Sauvagnac. "On the other hand, I'm sorry to say he's guilty of certain—equivocal activities."

"Henry?" said Kate, incredulous. "Never!"

"What is he alleged to have done, Colonel?" Eleanor asked.

"In the first place," said Sauvagnac, "it appears that he reached Europe by making use of a travel document to which he had no right. In the second place, there is reason to suspect that he's made away with a trunk containing, among other articles, an engagement ring and a miniature, both of great sentimental value."

"A ring?" said Kate, frowning. "And a miniature?"

"I further understand," said Sauvagnac, "that he chanced to remark, while conversing in a New York tavern called The Shamrock House, that if he ever reached Paris he intended to apply to the Lafayette Circle here for our influence in the furthering of his proclaimed military plans."

"Proclaimed?" said Eleanor.

"As a *result*," said Sauvagnac, "of that chance remark he made, I've just now had an urgent inquiry about him."

Kate said sturdily, "Colonel Sauvagnac, I'm sure there must be some perfectly simple explanation for all this."

"There is indeed, Miss Casteign. Excuse me." Sauvagnac strode to the double doors, threw them open. "Monsieur, will you step into the hall here?"

Henry Lane Duprez walked into the hall.

Seventeen

The tall young tobacco planter stopped dead. Sudden color flushed the convalescent pallor of his face as he gazed at Kate. No less unbelieving, she was gazing at him.

"Henry!"

"Kate? *Kate!*"

He strode to her.

"Providence," Kate breathed, close in the circle of his arms. "I knew it—oh, I *knew* you were close—my heart told me!"

Her arms tightened about him. He winced audibly. She looked up at him with instant anxiety.

"What is it? Henry, you're hurt—wounded—a Russian bullet—"

"No, an American one, from a derringer—"

"Henry! *I* was shot at, too, by a French bullet—but it missed. Oh, *why* didn't yours?"

"Don't worry," said Duprez. "The wound's almost healed."

They gazed at each other, miraculously reunited through a hail of lead.

"Kate," said Duprez, "the very scar is gone, banished by the sight of you, my love, my long-lost love—"

Their lips met.

Eleanor, standing stunned, said, "Colonel Sauvagnac, what does this mean?"

"This gentleman here, Miss Gerrard, is Mr. Henry Lane Duprez of New Orleans."

"Demonstrably so, it seems," said Eleanor. "But then— that other man, that extraordinary person that Sir Bartle Mole and I brought here—?"

"An impostor," Sauvagnac said grimly. "You have been imposed upon, Miss Gerrard, by an adventurer—what we call, here in France, a *chevalier d'industrie*—a busy gentleman of smooth address and no principles."

"I always *knew* there was something strange about that man!" Eleanor exclaimed. "Such peculiar eyes!"

"Alert for the main chance," said Sauvagnac. "Heaven knows what his game is, but, as I was advising the real Mr. Duprez here when you arrived, the best hope of running that industrious gentleman to earth might be to apply to General Aupick, to whom I unfortunately recommended the scoundrel. General Aupick's address is Number forty-four Rue Bourbon."

"The general, I regret to say," Caroline Aupick presently informed her three urgent visitors, "is not at home tonight. He always sleeps at his command post at the Invalides when some military duty requires him to be up and doing at a very early hour."

She had received the visitors in her salon. She was seated, as were Kate and Eleanor, the two girls still wearing their hats and mantles. Duprez was standing, ulstered, his tweed traveling cap in his hand.

"Never in *any* circumstances," said Caroline, "must the general be intruded upon when at the Invalides among his troops."

"Madame Aupick," said Duprez, "the man we seek is a dangerous impostor."

"And probably a lunatic," said Eleanor. "He seemed to *belong* among the gargoyles!"

"How could you have dreamed, Eleanor," said Kate, taking Duprez's hand, "that I'd fall in love with a gargoyle?"

"I'm extremely disturbed by what you've told me," said Caroline; "the more so as I've reason to know that my own son, Charles Baudelaire, is under this frightful individual's influence."

"Then they may even now be together," Kate said quickly.

"With this—this industrious gentleman, as Colonel Sauvagnac called him," said Eleanor, "tempting your son into some criminal act this very minute!"

"This is appalling," said Caroline. "Tell me, did you come here in a cab?"

"It waits at the door," said Duprez.

"Very well," said Caroline—and, provided now with a reason beyond question, even by General Aupick, for visiting her son's notorious apartment, she rose and pulled the bell rope beside the fireplace.

Opening her vanity case, she looked at her reflection in the pier glass over the mantel.

"Charles sometimes protests, as a young man will," she said, "that his mother is his only woman."

She applied her rouge pad, wishing that she had had more time to prepare for this surprise intrusion, late at night, into her son's private life as lived in his intimate circle of mysterious black woman and other lewd companions.

"I shall accompany you immediately," she said, "to Charles's apartment." The door opening then, to disclose the flunkey, she added, "Jean, tell Marie I require my evening cloak. The mauve one, tell her."

Looking at herself in the pier glass, she wondered if a touch more color on her lips would be advisable for an attractive woman about to be shocked into making a scene and exhibiting to her son the broken heart of a mother. But already her eyes were sparkling with anticipatory excitement, so she decided against gilding the lily, and, closing her vanity case after making sure there were a handkerchief and smelling salts in it, she turned bravely to her visitors.

"Let us go," she said. "Charles is living at the Hôtel Lauzun, in the Île Saint-Louis."

"Monsieur Baudelaire?" said the *concierge* at the Hôtel Lauzun.

"I wish to see him immediately. I," said Caroline, "am his mother. Take us directly to his apartment."

"Oh, madame," said the *concierge*, "I fear I have bad news for you."

Caroline felt a stab of real dismay. "What's happened?"

"Courage, madame!" said the *concierge*. "It's no worse than has befallen many a young gentleman of rank and fashion."

"Out with it, man," said Duprez. "What are you trying to tell us?"

"Monsieur Baudelaire, though in arrears with his rent," said the *concierge*, "still has his apartment here—but it stands empty."

"Empty?" Caroline exclaimed.

"Alas, madame, all his goods and chattels were removed some while ago on the petition of creditors. We've not set eyes on Monsieur Baudelaire since that unhappy event."

"Oh, Mr. Duprez," said Caroline, "I might of course have anticipated something of this kind." She could not help a feeling of pride at her son's romantic worldliness. "Really, Charles is quite the wickedest young spendthrift in Paris!"

Duprez asked the *concierge*, "Have you any idea where Monsieur Baudelaire might be found?"

"At this hour, monsieur, possibly at the Café Momus in the Rue des Prêtres."

"Thank you," said Duprez, giving the man a tip. "Come, Madame Aupick, let's join the girls in the cab."

As they moved away across the great old shadowy hall, the *concierge* glanced at his tip and, inspired by its transatlantic munificence, called after them, "M'sieur-dame—if he's not at the Momus, try the Café Procope."

"Thank you," Duprez called.

"Or the Rotonde in Montparnasse."

"Thank you."

"M'sieu, m'sieu—you might try the Bal d'Ossian, near the new Arch of Triumph."

"Thank you."

The door banged.

"Ugh!" said Baudelaire, with a shudder. "Rats!"

Rodent eyes, surprised by the sudden light of the lanthorn he held in a pink-gloved hand, glittered up at him for an instant with beady malevolence, then vanished as, with scurries, rustlings and swiftly slithering tails, the congregation of rats burrowed into dank straw on the loose-box floor.

"How can Crespigny have made a pet of one?" Baudelaire said, with revulsion. "Disgusting creatures, they were eating something—"

"Horse turds," said Poe, as he unbolted the lower half of the loose-box door.

Their shadows—Baudelaire's silk-hatted, Poe's with its loftier beaver—wheeled hugely, as they went in, over walls where mildewed horse blinkers, and harness collars with the stuffing leaking out, hung from wooden hooks.

"Damn this ammoniac reek," wheezed Poe, coughing. "Hang up the lanthorn, Charles."

"It's smudged my silk gloves," complained Baudelaire, as he obeyed.

"Smudge them further," said Poe, "by spreading that bit of horse blanket on the straw."

"I feel the rats are watching our every move," said Baudelaire, as with fastidious fingertips he pulled down the rag of blanket which dangled from a triangular manger high up in a corner, "Oh dear God," he added, as he spread the blanket on a turd-free part of the straw, "there's a gigantic spider scuttled out of it! Henri, we shall probably catch fleas, if nothing worse."

"I've seen better kept livery stables," Poe agreed, putting down the satchel he carried. "At West Point the stable floors are so spotless you could eat off them."

"Admirable," said Baudelaire, "but I think I'd rather starve." He added, as Poe took a watch from his greatcoat pocket, "A gold watch, Henri? I haven't seen that before."

"The night wears on," said Poe, ignoring Baudelaire's remark. "I want General Aupick to notice this distinctive fob."

Putting the watch, Henry Lane Duprez's twenty-first birthday gift from his father, into his vest pocket, Poe arranged the fob with care, then from his greatcoat pocket took Kate's ring box and extracted the ring.

"I also want the general to notice this ring," he said and, licking the little finger of his left hand, forced the ring onto it with a slight exertion of effort.

"My American," marveled Baudelaire, "a man of infinite resource!"

"The art of deception, Charles, depends on tremendous trifles."

"None could be more tremendous, Henri, than the loading of the pistols with blanks. Ancelle agreed to it at once. His relief was pathetic."

"His consternation, when the trap springs," said Poe, "will be pitiful in the extreme." Kneeling down on the horse blanket, he opened the satchel, took out a clean napkin. "Spread this on the blanket, Charles, while I unwrap the heart."

As Baudelaire, stooping, his gold-knobbed stick under his arm, spread the napkin, Poe pulled off the newspaper from a small bundle which he took from the satchel. A sheep's heart was revealed. He placed on the blanket the newspaper with the heart on it. Reaching for Baudelaire's stick, he unsheathed the rapier.

"Has this tasted blood, Charles?"

"Unfortunately, Henri, opportunity has been lacking."

"There's a first time for everything, Charles."

On the wall, the shadow of Poe's arm rose up huge, gripping the rapier, and stabbed downward.

Unskewering the heart, he wiped the rapier on the newspaper, sheathed the blade, returned the swordstick to Baudelaire.

His eyes gleaming, cavernous, Poe squeezed the heart. Blood dribbled copiously from it onto the white napkin.

"The sight of blood, Charles, prompts in the average mind an association with a wound. But such hasty deductions can of course be fallacious. There, that's enough blood, I think. Fold the napkin into a pad. I'll toss this now anemic organ out of the rats' reach."

Wrapping the heart in the newspaper, he tossed it up into the manger. From the satchel he drew out a white object, limp and furry, which he handed to Baudelaire.

"Poor Jeanne," said Baudelaire; "her ermine muff."

Poe took from the satchel a globular object swathed in napkins.

"And here's her little censer bowl, Charles, filled with smoldering charcoal and with the lid fixed firmly on. Handle it carefully—it's very hot."

Baudelaire took delivery of the bundle on Jeanne's muff, which, with his stick clamped under his arm, he held in both pink-gloved hands. Thus stooped, like a deferential *maître d'hô-tel* proffering a pineapple on a fur tray, he cast an uneasy glance back over his shoulder.

"Don't look now, Henri," he said, "but the king of all rats is climbing up to that heart in the manger!"

"First there," said Poe, "first served."

As he spoke, the clip-clopping of a horse's hoofs became audible. Approaching, growing louder, they rang suddenly on the cobbles of the stable yard. Wheels rumbled, candle lamps swam nimbused out of the mist, and a closed four-wheeler carriage rolled to a standstill just outside the open door of the loose-box.

"Sue and O'Neddy," said Baudelaire.

Eugène Sue, the established novelist, and Théophile Dondey, alias O'Neddy, who had yet to find a pornographic publisher for his erotic romances, climbed down from the box of the carriage.

"And the passenger?" Poe asked, rising from his knees.

"No problem," said Sue. "Not a word to say for himself."

Poe took the lanthorn from the hook where it hung, went out to the carriage.

"He's at our disposal till noon," Sue said, "then he must be returned to the contractor."

"In case Monsieur Laboine's ledger of the dead should be subjected to audit," said O'Neddy, with a flash of his glasses in the lanthorn light.

Poe opened the carriage door, thrust in his head and shoulders. The light of the lanthorn he held fell on the passenger seated in the carriage corner.

Poe froze, in shock.

The man in the corner was dressed in black, with a tall beaver hat. Eyes closed, chin on chest, pale face smoothly shaven except for a thin black moustache and a scald blemish still red on his left cheek, the man Poe crouched staring at was—Poe.

The opposite door of the carriage opened. Baudelaire, holding the ermine muff and the hot, napkin-wrapped censer bowl, thrust in his head. He, too, froze, his startled dark eyes on the silent passenger.

"Yes," he whispered, "yes—he's *you*, Henri!"

Poe swallowed with a dry throat. Arrogant as he was apt to be in the consciousness of his plot-making gift and the intellectual satisfaction of its exercise, yet what was morbidly intuitive in his temperament responded emotionally to the sight of this dead simulacrum of his living self.

"Israfel—" The puppet of the plot-maker? Or a ghost to shame the artist? That cleavage in Poe's temperament which was the bane of his existence held him clamped and staring. "There but for the grace of God . . ."

"Even to the scald mark on the cheek," said Baudelaire. "Henri, how did you get—your mark?"

The question released Poe from his momentary paralysis.

"I tempted the fair sex," he said, "with forbidden fire."

Coughing seized him. Clapping his handkerchief to his mouth, he stood the lanthorn on the coir matting of the carriage floor. Conquering the cough, and his more vulnerable self, he wheezed, "Charles, the muff."

Taking the muff, Poe pushed it up over the pauper's left hand and forearm, now growing limp with the diminution of rigor mortis. Poe took the napkin-wrapped censer bowl, forced the hot bundle into the muff and, with a handkerchief, tied the muff tightly at the dead profligate's wrist.

"That'll hold," he said.

"His last journey," said Baudelaire, fascinated.

"Last but one," said Poe, seeing for a moment the mud mounds of the Buttes Chaumont cemetery—potter's field.

Banishing that thought, he took up the lanthorn and drew back, closing the carriage door, leaving the window down.

Baudelaire came back around the carriage.

"The napkin pad, Charles," Poe said. "Give it to Sue."

Baudelaire, with pink-gloved fingertips, handed the folded napkin, wet with blood, to Sue, who put it into the medical bag he carried, then dropped the bag through the window into the carriage, with the passenger seated silent there in his eternal night.

"Well, gentlemen?" said Poe. The more commanding, the more icily arrogant for his moment of weak compunction, he took off his West Point greatcoat, folded it, dropped it in through the carriage window. He stood tall, in black, with his lofty hat. "Now, sirs—we all know our drill, I think?"

They nodded, a shadowy group here by the carriage glimmering sleekly black in the light of the lanthorn light held by O'Neddy.

"You, Charles?" Poe said. "Your brief is clear?"

Baudelaire said, "I hire a saddle horse from the livery stable here, make my own way to the Bois de Boulogne, and then—"

"At the appropriate moment," Poe said, "you, the unseen witness, loudly crack a dead stick."

"That's all?"

"That, Charles, is all."

Sue drew a flask from his pocket. "Have we time for a drink?"

Poe looked about him. Except for the gleam of the lanthorn and the carriage candle lamps, there was only mist and dead of night.

"The plan's made, every factor in the situation evaluated and deftly utilized. A drink?" said Poe. "Willingly!"

Eighteen

The majestic bulk of the Arc de Triomphe loomed hugely in the night mist. No cock had yet crowed from backyards in the adjacent maze of narrow streets when Armand Crespigny, the epicene composer with the cauterized nose, took his new pet to show off to the *habitués* of the only establishment in the area that provided diversion for the insomniac.

"You will be much admired here, pet," said Crespigny, leading the urchin boy by a long ribbon tied around his neck. "It's a famous *boîte de nuit* called the Bal d'Ossian. Do you know why?"

"I'm hungry," his pet whined.

"You are very ignorant, pet," said Crespigny chidingly.

"It is called the Bal d'Ossian because all this *quartier* reflects the influence of the Emperor Napoleon, and Ossian was his favorite author. History fails to record the name of his favorite composer. No doubt his works were atrociously banal."

The Bal d'Ossian was smoky and crowded, filled with a din of voices and the rattling of tambourines shaken by a troupe of dancing girls whose pirouettes and high kicks on a small dais displayed fanciful garters under their petticoats but an evident absence of more relevant lingerie.

Dressed like a muzhik fresh in from the steppes, an astrakhan hat jaunty on his head, his nose elongated like Cyrano de Bergerac's because of a surgical dressing on it, Crespigny led his pet to the bar presided over by a spangled lady who, embowered in bottles, leaned with her powdered bosom mounded upon the counter for the easier inspection of two elegant revelers whose confident tones and incomprehensible French marked them as members of the English nobility.

"Monsieur Crespigny," said the spangled lady, raising her brows, "what's that you have there?"

"I've brought my new pet to show you, Hortense," said the composer. "Isn't it sweet? I found it curled up under one of those stone benches in the Tuileries Gardens. Such a darling little stray, it seemed a pity to let it be seized by ruffians. They do horrid things to little strays!"

"Good God!" said one of the Englishmen, screwing a monocle into his eye for a better look at the composer and his pet.

"Come, pet," said Crespigny, tugging on the ribbon, "don't be shy! There, Hortense—isn't it charming? I took it home and put it in the little suit I used to look so enchanting in myself."

The captive gamin, whose bare feet and legs were encrusted with dirt though he wore a suit of plum-colored velvet with mother-of-pearl buttons and a crochetwork collar, gazed with eyes that gleamed through his grubby hair at the array of sweetmeats on the counter.

"I'm hungry, m'sieu," he complained, licking snot from his upper lip.

"Now, now," chided Crespigny, "it mustn't be a *greedy* pet—must it, Hortense?"

But an attractive lady in a mauve evening cloak, escorted by a tall young man wearing a tweed ulster and traveling cap, came in from the street with an air of urgency, and Hortense, ceasing to lean on the counter, plumped up her breasts hospitably for the receipt of custom.

"M'sieu, -'dame?" she said.

The newcomers, Caroline Aupick and Henry Lane Duprez, glanced about them at the gaudy, noisy and smoky scene, and Caroline asked Hortense, "Do you know a Monsieur Charles Baudelaire by sight?"

"Possibly, madame," replied Hortense, with professional caution, "but then again, possibly not. One sees so many faces by sight. May one have the honor of knowing who it is who inquires?"

"I," said Caroline, "am Monsieur Baudelaire's mother."

Armand Crespigny's bandaged nose, elongated like an anteater's, turned slowly in Caroline's direction.

"*Mes compliments,* madame," said Hortense, "but no— Monsieur Baudelaire is not here tonight."

Caroline and Duprez looked at each other.

"*Pardon,*" said Crespigny. In his eyes was a viper gleam. He fingered his nose with tender reminiscence. He had a score to settle, and here were the means delivered into his musicianly hands. "*Pardon,* madame—did I hear you say you are Charles Baudelaire's mother?"

"I am indeed, sir," said Caroline. "Do you know my son?"

"Do I know him?" said Crespigny, amused. "Do I know Charles Baudelaire? Madame, I know Charles as well as I know my own nose." He bowed, lifting his astrakhan hat. "This is a most unexpected pleasure. Charles's *mother!*"

"Have you any idea," asked Caroline, "where he's to be found?"

"Or," added Duprez, "his American—associate?"

"Ah, his American," said Crespigny, reveling in the situation. "Baudelaire's American! Such dear boys—quite inseparable, these days. Why, yes, I think I know where they're likely to be found—oh, I certainly think I could hazard an intelligent guess."

"Then please do so," said Caroline.

But it was well known in aesthetic circles that Baudelaire was at pains to keep his mother and his black mistress unacquainted with each other, and Armand Crespigny, left cruelly abandoned in the Luxembourg Gardens, was in no hurry to forego the savor of revenge.

"Does Charles Baudelaire's mother," he fluted sweetly, "keep pets—other, of course, than dear Charles himself? They are not *always* a comfort, to be sure"—he fingered his bandaged nose—"but I should be quite lost without one. Do you like my latest? I'm going to call it Caniche." He pulled the gamin closer with the ribbon lead. "There, Caniche—make a leg to Monsieur Baudelaire's beautiful mother."

"I'm hungry," sniveled the captive.

Caroline said tensely, "Monsieur—"

"Some pets, of course," said Crespigny, "have nasty habits —like pinching with claws, or biting. Such pets are to be avoided. But *my* pet is the perfect pet. I must—I simply must show you why I adopted it when I found it astray in the Tuileries Gardens."

He tilted the boy's head back by its tangled hair, wiped away the snot with the boy's crochetwork collar.

"Open, pet," begged the composer. "Open wide, Caniche— for Monsieur Baudelaire's enchanting mama!"

The boy gaped open his mouth.

"There, isn't that a charming sight?" said Crespigny. "You see? It's lost all its milk teeth, and its vicious great fangs haven't come bursting through its pretty pink gums yet. There's just this one nasty little tooth left in front—"

"Monsieur," said Caroline, her kid-gloved hands tensely opening and closing, "we've traversed half of Paris, from one night haunt to another, looking for my son. If you know where he's to be found, I do beg you—"

"In a moment, madame," said Crespigny. "Poor little Caniche is hungry. We mustn't be cruel to our pets, must we? We must *feed* them. Does my pet fancy the nice creamy *gâteau* on the counter?"

The boy, mouth gaping open in Crespigny's clutch, tried to nod eagerly.

"And is this," said Crespigny, wiggling with finger and thumb the boy's solitary tooth, which was somewhat loose, "—is this my pet's *sweet* tooth?"

The boy gurgled, possibly in acquiescence.

"Well," said Crespigny, extracting the tooth with a sharp jerk, "it's gone now, pet!"

The boy gave an anguished cry, largely drowned by the whoops and shrieks of the dancing girls as they quit the small stage, arm in arm, pirouetting their button boots and kicking up their petticoats.

"Good God!" said the Englishman with the monocle, staring at the blood-tipped tooth held up by Crespigny. "What unfeeling cads these Russians are!"

His companion nodded grimly.

The boy wiped his mouth with the back of his hand, looked at the blood smear left on the hand, and whined, "I'm hungry!"

Duprez, tight-lipped, took a step toward Crespigny. "Now, see here, sir—"

"Oh, yes," said Crespigny. "Well, we mustn't keep Charles Baudelaire's lovely mother waiting, must we?" He tossed the tooth into a bowl of fruit *compote* on the counter, and turned to Caroline. "Dear lady, you will find Charles, I feel quite sure, at Number seven Place Dauphine, in the fifth-floor apartment of his *exquisite* mistress. His American will be there, too. The three will doubtless be indulging in an oriental pastime for which they have a mutual taste. And do, please,'' said Crespigny, with fiendish glee, ''do *please* inform dear Charles that Armand Crespigny —note the name, madame—did his poor best to be of assistance to you.''

''Come, Madame Aupick,'' said Duprez.

''But this child's hungry,'' said Caroline—and, taking from the counter the plate bearing the large *gâteau*, gave the boy one of the slices already cut.

Seizing it, the boy sank ravenous gums into the creamy segment.

''How kind!'' beamed Crespigny. ''How thoughtfully feminine of Baudelaire's mother to feed my pet—''

''And not neglect *you*, monsieur,'' said Caroline pleasantly; and, holding the plate in both her kid-gloved hands, jammed the major portion of the *gâteau*, including its dish, straight into the composer's face.

Thoughtfully feminine, Caroline stood watching as the plate, glutinously freeing itself from its recent contents, slid down Crespigny's face and shattered on the floor, leaving the composer, apparently immobilized by shock, with his augmented nose protruding like a sundial's gnomon from a clotted mask.

Availing himself of a lull occasioned by general surprise, all eyes being fixed in fascination on Crespigny, the boy grabbed from the counter a double handful of sweetmeats and, the ribbon fluttering from his neck at the speed of his departure, escaped into the night.

Caroline said, with hauteur, ''*Au revoir*, Monsieur Crespigny.''

Taking Duprez's arm, she swept out with him to the waiting cab.

''Where now?'' said the cabman.

''Place Dauphine,'' said Duprez curtly.

Following Caroline, he joined Kate and Eleanor in the cab.

As it jingled off, scream after scream rang out from a demented pet fancier in the Bal d'Ossian.

"Heavens," said Kate, "did something happen?"

"*Allez,*" said Jeanne Duval, as the bell in the little lobby of her love nest sounded a silvery tinkle.

Charcoal smoldered on a brass plate on the low coffee table in her salon. Seated in the lotus-seat manner among the cushions on her ottoman, and lightly clad in transparent negligee and numerous bangles, with her hair unbound, she was leaning forward to blow with beestung lips on the charcoal, in the process of beguiling her solitude with another pipe or two.

Again the bell tinkled a silvery summons.

"*Zut alors!*" said Jeanne.

Faint feathers of smoke drifted about the flickering wicks that floated in the scented oil of her harem lamps, and the gorilla's head leered lewdly from its quilted wall niche, as she unfolded her legs with a jingle of anklets and rose with a ballet dancer's easy grace.

Again, insistently, the bell tinkled.

"*Nom d'une pipe,*" murmured Jeanne.

Taking up one of the lamps, she moved dreamily through the bead curtain into the diminutive lobby, thickly carpeted, with walls lacquered in crimson and gold.

Drawing the silver bolt of the front door, she opened it a crack and hazily beheld on the landing a lady in a mauve cloak with a hood, a tall young man wearing an ulster and holding a traveling cap, and two younger ladies.

"*Mon Dieu,* a deputation," said Jeanne. "What do you want?"

Caroline ran a patrician gaze over Jeanne, from her bare feet with their silver-painted toenails, to the ebon charms of her perfect body, indifferently concealed, and her orgiastic hair.

"'Mademoiselle Jeanne Duval,'" said Caroline, reading, quite unnecessarily, from the card slotted on the red-lacquered front door, "'Danseuse du Théâtre'?"

"C'est moi," said Jeanne.

"We are looking," Caroline said coldly, "for Monsieur Charles Baudelaire."

"Not here," said Jeanne.

"We are reliably informed," said Caroline, "otherwise."

"Too bad," said Jeanne languidly. "Good-bye."

She started to close the door, but Duprez intruded the peremptory foot of a tobacco planter with seigneurial rights over black girls, demanding, "Has he been here tonight with his American . . . associate?"

"Earlier," said Jeanne. "Gone now—away on business. Good-bye."

"Where have they gone?" Caroline said sharply. "And on what business?"

But Jeanne's eyes, hazily amber, the pupils contracted from conference with the poppy, were blinking now at Kate and Eleanor, who had thought it advisable to attend upon Caroline lest she be overcome by finding her son in some sodden debauch, which the girls would in any case have been sorry to miss seeing for their broader education.

"You," said Jeanne, blinking her eyes into focus on Kate. "Let me look at you—"

She held her lamp of a foolish virgin, which she was far from being, closer to Kate's face.

"I know that face," said Jeanne.

"I'm sure," said Kate, with dignity, "we have never met."

"Fair hair," mused Jeanne, "gray eyes. Mais oui! Nameless lady! Come, I have something for you."

"What can she mean, Henry?" Kate said, taking Duprez's hand as Jeanne beckoned her to enter. "Something for me?"

"Let us see," said Caroline, and swept into the lobby.

The others followed. Jeanne was going into the salon. The

bead curtain swayed to behind her. Caroline paused, sniffing the air.

"Some heathen incense," she said.

From the salon, Jeanne called, "Come, nameless lady!"

Caroline, followed by Duprez and the girls, passed through the bead curtain into the salon. Caroline stopped abruptly, her eyes on the coffee table with its glowing charcoal and litter of bamboo pipes.

"Opium," she said. "An opium den! I might have known it! This explains so much of Charles's behavior."

Jeanne turned, looking at Kate. "Here, this is for you, nameless lady."

"My *miniature?*" said Kate, taking it from Jeanne's proffered hand. "Look, Henry, it's the miniature I gave you!"

"So he's been here," Duprez said grimly, "—the American who's using my name." He demanded of Jeanne, "Where is the ring?"

"Who knows?" said Jeanne, uninterested. "Go away now." She stretched voluptuously, her bangles tinkling. "Oh, I'm sleepy. All go away. Good-bye."

"Mademoiselle Duval," said Caroline, "I am here in quest of Charles Baudelaire, and I intend to find him. I am Madame Aupick, his mother."

"Oooooh," yawned Jeanne, her head in the clouds, and the clouds in her head, "how sleeeepy I am!"

"Mademoiselle," said Caroline dangerously, "are you so steeped in noxious fumes that you did not hear what I said?"

"I heard," said Jeanne, coming down to earth briefly, but with dignity. "And I'm surprised that *you*, madame, should come here. It is not customary."

"I *beg* your pardon?" said Caroline.

"Such behavior is not expected," said Jeanne, "from a well-bred son's mother."

"When I feel myself in need of correction in maternal deportment," said Caroline, her kid-gloved hands tautly opening and closing, "I shall not seek it from concubines accustomed to the manners of equatorial harems."

"Oh, *la, la!*" said Jeanne.

"Mademoiselle," said Caroline, "if you know where Charles Baudelaire is, I earnestly advise you, for your own sake, to tell me—this instant!"

"Then you will go away?" said Jeanne, cloudily hopeful.

"Then," said Caroline, "and not before."

"Charles has gone to the Bois de Boulogne," said Jeanne, "to fight a duel."

"A duel?" Caroline froze.

"With General Aupick," said Jeanne vaguely.

Caroline saw Death reach out with a cold finger to touch— her son.

Nineteen

Baudelaire, in the faint dilution of darkness which presaged the dawn, was riding his horse at a slow walk along a grassy ride walled by laurel thickets and tall trees.

Silk-hatted, caped, with his pink-gloved hands gripping the bridle and his gold-knobbed stick, he peered through the impeding foliage to his left—and he caught sight there at last, and at no great distance, of a glimmer of candle lamps.

He checked his horse, dismounted, and led it, brushing against the laurels and shaking the night's mist drops from the young leaves of spring, toward the candle lamp glimmer. Tying the horse's bridle to the low-sweeping branch of a tree, he walked forward, crouching a little, over soft ground, until he could make out that the lamps burned on a carriage dimly discernible to him as a dark outline through the laurels.

He paused, listening. All was still. He whistled, quietly, the opening phrases of *"Auprès de ma blonde."*

Poe and O'Neddy heard it. They were standing by the carriage, which was stationary, drawn up close in under the trees.

O'Neddy murmured, "Baudelaire's arrived."

Poe nodded. Quietly, he whistled the next phrase of the tune, and the concluding phrase answered from the wood. Poe opened the glass of one of the lamps. The candlelight glinted momentarily on the ring on the little finger of his left hand, and on the watch fob on his vest, as he blew out the candle. Moving around in front of the horse, which stood munching in its nosebag, he blew out the other candle lamp and returned, a black-clad figure with stovepipe hat, to O'Neddy's side.

"Day begins to pale," murmured the erotic novelist.

Again Poe nodded. Taking gradually perceptible shape now was a strip of greensward, about eighty yards wide, walled between facing ramparts of dark, tall trees interspersed with thickets of laurel. A faint mist hung dankly over the grass.

"The mist dims my glasses," said O'Neddy, taking them off.

"According to plan," said Poe.

Blinking myopically as he polished his glasses, O'Neddy chuckled, "Master of mysteries, sultan of stratagems!"

"A mere logician," said Poe, with a shrug.

"Listen," said O'Neddy.

The hoof thuds of a horse, drumming at a trot on turf, became audible, approaching. Through the mist, candle lamps swam into view and, to a jingle of harness, a closed carriage came on along the length of the greensward between the tree ramparts.

"Aupick and Ancelle on the box," murmured O'Neddy; "Aupick holding the reins."

"Would you expect otherwise?" said Poe, and, in the dank air, coughed into his handkerchief.

"Sue will have been watching for them to pass," said O'Neddy.

"Timing is of the essence," Poe said, wheezing slightly.

"Aupick's spotted us," said O'Neddy. "He's pulling over to draw up on the opposite side of the greensward."

"That," Poe said, "is why we got here first."

"You guessed he'd keep his distance from you?" O'Neddy said admiringly.

Poe shrugged. "I never guess."

Baudelaire, lurking in the wood behind Poe and O'Neddy, was searching around for a dead stick. He rejected several before finding one suitable to his purpose, as briefed by his American.

Baudelaire leaned the stick against the trunk of a tree. He leaned the stick at several different angles, decided on the most effective and, leaving the stick thus sloped, peered again through the interstices of the laurels at the dark shape of the carriage. He could hear the murmuring voices of Poe and O'Neddy.

"Aupick's a handsome man," said O'Neddy.

General Aupick, on the far side of the greensward, which was growing with every minute more clearly defined, was lighting a cheroot at one of the lamps of his carriage. His man of law, Monsieur Ancelle, was buckling a nosebag on the horse. Aupick blew out the carriage lamps.

"Not only is he a handsome man," Poe said, "but he has the mediocre thought processes which mark him as ideal ambassador material."

"Here comes Sue," said O'Neddy.

The lamps of another carriage were approaching, through the fast-thinning mist, along the greensward. Eugène Sue, holding the reins, was alone on the box, his silent passenger unseen in the dark interior of the closed carriage.

Keeping to that side of the greensward where Poe and

O'Neddy were standing, Sue drove past quite close to them and pulled up some twenty or so yards farther on, close in under the trees and parallel with them.

With the mahogany pistol box under his arm, Sue climbed down from the driving seat, blew out the lamps of his carriage, then strode out to the center of the greensward.

Standing there, silk-hatted and caped, in the gray but growing light, he glanced across at General Aupick and Monsieur Ancelle, on one side of the greensward, then at Poe and O'Neddy, on the other.

"Gentlemen!" Sue's voice rang loud and clear in the stillness. "I now formally ask you—have you arrived at a composition of this affair?"

No answer from either side of the greensward.

"Very well," said Sue. "We proceed."

He laid a folded white handkerchief on the grass, which had been nibbled short by sheep. The box under his arm, he stepped out ten measured paces, laid another folded handkerchief on the grass. He straightened.

"Seconds, please!"

Sue's summons, in the dawn hush, was clearly heard by Baudelaire where he lurked, an unseen witness, in the wood. Peering intently through the laurels, he saw O'Neddy and the lawyer Ancelle join Sue in the center of the greensward, between the handkerchiefs that lay, small white squares, on the grass.

"Now, gentlemen"—again Sue's voice, crisp and clear, reached Baudelaire—"I lay this box on the turf. I unlock it. Under your surveillance, I load first *this* pistol—so—and return it to the box."

In the wood, Baudelaire lifted his left foot, poising it above the dead stick that leaned against the tree trunk.

Again, Sue's voice sounded, from out on the greensward: "I now load *this* pistol—so—and return it to the box."

Baudelaire stamped his foot down hard on the leaning stick, which snapped with a loud crack.

Sue's voice rang out: "What was that? We want no interlopers. Gentlemen, remain here. Keep an eye on that box."

Peering through the laurels, Baudelaire saw O'Neddy, standing beside Monsieur Ancelle out there in the center of the greensward, take off his glasses to polish them.

Sue came striding toward the trees. Stopping short of their towering rampart, he called peremptorily into the wood, "Who's there?"

Baudelaire stood silent, faintly smiling.

"Anybody there?" Sue called sharply.

Deep in the wood, a jay cackled derisively.

Peering through the laurel thicket, Baudelaire saw Sue turn and stride back to join O'Neddy and the lawyer in the center of the greensward.

Again Sue's voice reached Baudelaire: "A false alarm, Monsieur Ancelle, Monsieur Dondey—just a branch cracked, I think. But we'd better press on, before the world's astir. The light's good enough now, there's not a breath of wind, conditions could hardly be better." He picked up the pistol box from the turf. "Gentlemen, call your principals."

Ancelle called, "General Aupick!"

O'Neddy called, "Monsieur Duprez!"

General Aupick and Poe strode out, from opposite sides, to the center of the greensward.

Sue's voice, crisp and commanding, reached Baudelaire: "Now, gentlemen, there's no light advantage in either direction. General Aupick, that handkerchief marks your station. Monsieur Duprez, that other handkerchief marks yours. I now ask you to stand, here on this spot between the handkerchiefs, back to back."

Watching intently between the damp tangle of the laurels, Baudelaire saw General Aupick toss aside his cheroot and, taking off his ulster, hand it to Monsieur Ancelle, who folded it reverently over his arm. General Aupick, who was wearing civilian clothes and a silk hat, took up the commanded position, back to back with Poe in his high beaver hat.

"Take your weapon, General," said Sue, proffering the pistol box.

Watching from the wood, Baudelaire saw Aupick take a pistol, saw Sue move around to face Poe, who took the other pistol.

Sue snapped shut the box, stepped back. His voice rang out:

"On the word 'March,' you will go to your stations. On the word 'Turn,' you will turn. On the word 'Fire,' you will fire at your own discretion. Understood?"

"Understood."

"March!"

The duelers marched to their stations—and halted.

"Turn!"

The duelers turned, facing each other, raising their pistols at arm's length to the aim.

"Fire!"

A needle of flame spat from Aupick's pistol, the report of the discharge followed instantly by the frenzied chirrup of a fleeing blackbird.

Poe's knees buckled. He pitched forward.

"Beautiful," murmured Baudelaire, watching intently from the laurels. "Beautiful, Henri!"

Sue and O'Neddy ran to the fallen duelist.

"Lift him, Monsieur Dondey," Sue snapped at O'Neddy. "We'll get him to my carriage."

General Aupick slowly lowered his pistol. He turned to Monsieur Ancelle, who, thunderstruck, stood staring at Sue and O'Neddy as, each pulling around his neck an arm of Poe's, they heaved him up and bore him, with his head in its stovepipe hat lolling limply forward and his feet helplessly dragging, toward Sue's carriage.

General Aupick handed his pistol to Monsieur Ancelle, who took it and relinquished the General's ulster like a man in a trance.

General Aupick, donning his ulster, his work satisfactorily completed, walked over to his own carriage on the far side of the greensward.

Watching through the laurels, Baudelaire, exultant, saw Monsieur Ancelle look at the pistol in his hand as though momentarily expecting the firearm to explode again, this time in his face.

Baudelaire heard Sue's voice saying, "Carefully, Monsieur Dondey, handle him carefully," and knew that Sue and O'Neddy were lifting Poe into Sue's carriage, just the other side of the laurels there.

"Masterly," murmured Baudelaire to himself.

On the far side of the greensward, General Aupick was standing by his carriage, lighting a fresh cheroot. His second, Monsieur Ancelle, seemed to have taken root in the center of the greensward. He looked about him at the grass, the facing ramparts of tall trees, and up at the steadily paling sky, as though expecting Mother Nature to provide him with an explanation of an impossible occurrence. None being forthcoming, he looked again at the pistol he held as if it were Aaron's rod and might at any second turn into a wriggling serpent.

Suddenly, close to Baudelaire, a rustling sounded among the laurels, and a voice said softly, "Charles?"

"Here," Baudelaire whispered. "Here I am, Henri!"

Poe, crouching, now carrying his West Point greatcoat, which he had put into Sue's carriage at the livery stables, joined Baudelaire stealthily.

"Did they spot it, Charles?" Poe whispered, his eyes gleaming, dark-circled in the pallor of his face. "My transit through Sue's carriage—lifted in on the greensward side, ducking out here on the trees side?"

"They saw absolutely nothing of it, Henri!"

"Excellent, Charles, excellent! Sue's now bedecking poor Israfel with the ring and the watch and fob, tucking the muff and the hot censer bowl into the medical bag, and making appropriate use of the blood-stained napkin. Watch, Charles! Listen! In a moment now, our trap will spring!''

Crouched side by side, they peered through the tangle of the laurels.

General Aupick's voice rang out, calling, ''Ancelle!''

The lawyer, in the center of the greensward, turned slowly.

O'Neddy's voice rang out, shrill with outrage, ''A blank! Monsieur Sue—look here! A blank!''

The lawyer, halted in his tracks, turned back.

''Foul play!'' yelled O'Neddy. ''Monsieur Sue, look at this cartridge I've just taken from Duprez's unfired pistol. Look at it, Monsieur Sue—it's blank!'

''Sublime, Henri,'' Baudelaire whispered. ''Sublime!''

''General Aupick's heard,'' murmured Poe.

They peered through the laurel tangle. Aupick, every inch a general, came striding across the greensward, tottered after by Ancelle in his nightmare of bewilderment.

''Monsieur Sue,'' Aupick said harshly, ''what is this shouting about?''

Poe and Baudelaire crept cautiously to an angle from which they could see, through the laurel thicket, the greensward side of Sue's carriage.

''General Aupick,'' said Eugène Sue, ''your opponent is dead. Here—feel his wrist.''

He pulled the pauper's left arm out through the window of the carriage door. The ring glinted, diamond-bright, on the little finger of the pauper's hand. General Aupick gripped the wrist.

He grunted, ''H'm! Yes. No pulse.''

''And cooling rapidly,'' said Sue.

The general nodded grimly, releasing the dead man's wrist.

In the concealment of the thicket, Baudelaire pressed Poe's shoulder with a pink-gloved hand, breathing, ''My American—consummate master—Prince of the Pregnant Particular!''

''Shh,'' warned Poe. ''Listen!''

O'Neddy said bitterly, "You got your man, General Aupick."

"I had every intention of doing so," said the general.

"By foul play?" shouted O'Neddy, incensed.

"Monsieur Dondey, if it were not for your youth and eye-glasses," General Aupick said bitingly, "I would call you to instant account for that remark."

"And rightly so," said Eugène Sue. "Monsieur Dondey, guard your tongue. It's inconceivable that General Aupick could have connived at deception in an affair of honor."

"*There's* the culprit!" yelled O'Neddy. "There stands the guilty man—*that canting lawyer!*"

"Me?" Confronted by O'Neddy's accusing forefinger and eyes greatly magnified by thick lenses and outrage, Monsieur Ancelle emerged with a start from his nightmare trance. "No, no! How could—what do you . . . General, General—"

"He's the general's hired bootlicker!" raved O'Neddy. "He knows the general's habits, Monsieur Sue. He could *well* have known which pistol the general, with challenged's first choice, would take from the box—the upper or the lower!"

"Fantastic!" cried Ancelle. "This borders on lunacy! Messieurs—General—"

"It's obvious," shouted O'Neddy. "The carping craven was quivering in his breeches at the thought of his lucrative client being killed! The pistol box was lying open on the turf, Monsieur Sue, when you went to investigate that sound from the wood. Your back was turned. He was standing right beside the box. *That's* when he changed the cartridge for this blank!"

"Impossible!" screamed the lawyer. "Monsieur Dondey, you yourself were standing close by me—"

"I had my glasses off," shouted the erotic novelist. "They were misted, Monsieur Sue. I was polishing them. He seized his chance. Monsieur Sue, I'm as blind as a bat with my glasses off!"

Poe and Baudelaire, crouched behind the laurel thicket, exchanged a glance. Baudelaire shook his head helplessly, almost speechless with admiration, scarcely able to murmur, "Wizard of Wile!"

"Mere coordination," Poe whispered, "of observed phenomena. Shh, Charles! Listen!"

General Aupick's voice reached them: "Monsieur Ancelle —*have* you been guilty of any deception in this affair?"

The lawyer stood aghast.

"You see, Charles," Poe whispered, "how the web enmeshes him? He *is* guilty of deception—he agreed to the loading of the pistols with blanks. Culpability is now written all over him!"

"*Well,* sir?" General Aupick said dangerously.

"General—General," stammered the bedeviled advocate, "let me explain—"

"*Explain?* Answer the question, sir!" thundered the general. "Have you or have you not been guilty of deception?"

Ancelle, trembling, bleated, "General—in a sense—with the best intentions—"

"That's enough!" General Aupick exploded. "Get out of my sight!"

"I implore you," Ancelle wept. "General, a moment's grace —there's more—more here than meets the eye. General, please—"

General Aupick roared, *"Go!"* He seized the horsewhip from the socket beside the driving seat of Sue's carriage. "Get out of my sight, you legal nincompoop, before I flay you alive!"

Ancelle backed away, in haste and tears, helpless, appalled, his world tumbling in ruins around him.

"My God!" Baudelaire breathed, overwhelmed. "My God, Henri!"

"According to plan," Poe murmured, his eyes gleaming. "Shh, Charles! We approach the crux."

Sue's voice reached them, speaking most gravely, "General Aupick, this is disastrous, sir. You have political enemies, I believe?"

"I have indeed," Aupick said harshly.

"If this affair should leak out," said Sue, "they will hardly be likely to acquit you of collusion."

"Acquit me?" said Aupick. "No, by God, they'll make a crying scandal of this in the chancelleries! This will cost me an ambassadorship."

He hurled down the horsewhip in an access of savagery.

Sue said slowly, "*Need* the affair become known? In the circumstances, I'm prepared to promise you my own silence, and doubtless you can yourself ensure that your man of law, so little accustomed to encounters between gentlemen, is made to appreciate to the full the enormity of his behavior."

"I'll cut out his claptrapping tongue," said General Aupick.

"Which leaves," said Eugène Sue, "just *you*, Monsieur Dondey—"

O'Neddy, polishing his glasses, blinked his myopic eyes malevolently.

"Ancelle," said the erotic novelist, "should be publicly guillotined as a spectacle for the canaille. But—very well," he conceded sullenly, "my mouth is sealed, in the circumstances."

"So, then," said Sue. "We have here, in this carriage, the body of a roving American, a mere soldier of fortune, a mercenary who appeared out of the blue and can vanish into it—unremarked."

"Unremarked?" said General Aupick.

"I am a medical man, General," said Sue. "As such, I am conversant with—ways and means. I *could* arrange for the disposal of this corpse, and no one the wiser."

Crouched behind the laurel thicket, Poe murmured, "The crux, Charles. See how Aupick hesitates? A study in indecision! If he now agrees to the disposal of the body, he's doomed. You can call on him later today, when the body will be gone forever—"

"Nameless clay," Baudelaire whispered, "in the Buttes Chaumont cemetery—"

"And a mere number," Poe murmured, "in Monsieur Laboine's ledger of the pauper dead. But the ghost will rise to confront General Aupick when *you,* the unseen witness here, reveal that you saw him shoot down an unarmed man, then connive at the clandestine disposal of the body. And *you* have given no promise of silence—"

"But I could be persuaded," Baudelaire whispered, exultant, "for my mother's sake—*provided* Aupick consents to the release of my patrimony. Genius, Henri!"

"Justice," Poe said. "He forced you into the sequestration agreement. You now force him into its dissolution. A bargain for a bargain! Look at his face, Charles! His future's at stake. He knows it. His ambassadorship to Madrid or the Sublime Porte hangs upon a nod of his head."

"Oh, God," Baudelaire breathed, "he wavers!"

"He'll consent. He *must!*" Poe's eyes gleamed, his fingers clenched hard on Baudelaire's shoulder. "I have him trapped!"

Sue's voice reached them, crisp and urgent, through the laurel tangle:

"General Aupick, the sun rises. The world will soon be afoot. Am I to dispose of your victim? *Well,* sir? Your orders?"

"Now," Baudelaire whispered, tense, "or never—"

Through the laurel tangle they saw General Aupick slowly lift his hands—and let them fall.

"He yields," Poe breathed. "He has no option. Victory, Charles! Ah, sweet success!"

General Aupick's voice, heavy with surrender, reached them through the interstices of the thicket:

"Monsieur Sue, in the circumstances—all things considered—"

On Baudelaire's shoulder, Poe's fingers gripped like a vise. On Poe's lips was the smile of the logician triumphant, the apotheosis of the master plot weaver of "The Gold Bug."

But General Aupick's sentence remained unfinished.

A thudding of hoofs on turf was growing rapidly louder.

Twenty

The sun was up. The tall trees cast shadows, mile-long, down the sweep of greensward sparkling with dew between the facing ramparts of the wood.

General Aupick, Eugène Sue and O'Neddy stood struck to immobility, staring along the greensward.

To Poe and Baudelaire, crouched in the concealment of the laurel thickets, the drumming of approaching hoofs and the jingle of harness materialized into sudden view as a four-wheeler cab with the horse at a gallop, the cab wheels bouncing over undulations in the turf.

"Who comes?" Baudelaire breathed.

"Whoa! Whoa!" shouted the cabman, hauling back on his reins.

The horse slowed to a canter, a trot. The cab rolled to a standstill. The door opened. A young man ducked out. He wore an ulster and a traveling cap.

On Baudelaire's shoulder the grip of Poe's fingers slackened—and fell away. He recognized the young man in the ulster.

Baudelaire was peering tensely through the laurel tangle. He saw the young man in the ulster open the cab door. A woman in a mauve cloak stepped out, putting back her hood.

"My mother," Baudelaire breathed. "Henri, it's my mother—"

But Poe did not answer.

General Aupick's voice rang out, startled: "Caroline! What brings *you* here?"

"Charles!" she said. Baudelaire saw that two young girls had followed her out of the cab. "Where is Charles?"

She was looking around, quickly, searchingly, with intense anxiety—at Aupick, at Sue and O'Neddy, at Monsieur Ancelle standing staring near the carriage on the far side of the sward, still with the pistol in his hand.

Aupick said harshly, "How should *I* know where your son is?"

"What's happened here?" Her voice soared. "What have you done to Charles?"

"Oh, God!" Bandelaire breathed, peering tensely through the thicket. "Oh, God, Henri!"

But no answer came from Poe. And Baudelaire saw his mother move quickly forward over the grass, pointing at Sue's carriage.

"That arm—hanging there from the window!" Caroline said shrilly. "Whose arm is that? *Tell* me!"

General Aupick stepped quickly in front of her. "Stop! Stand back! Charles is not here, Caroline, you have my word for it. Why *should* he be?"

"I was told—"

· *196* ·

"I don't care what you were told! Your son is *not* here!"
Aupick controlled himself with a visible effort. "Now, Caroline,
I do not wish *you* here, either. Get back into that cab with your
companions and leave this place instantly!"

The young man in the ulster walked forward.

"General Aupick, sir—"

"Who the devil are you?" Aupick demanded.

"I am Henry Lane Duprez, sir, of New Orleans."

Baudelaire, crouched in the thickets, felt as though he had
been struck between the eyes.

He breathed, "Duprez? Henri, what does he mean?"

He looked to his side for the man who had been crouched
there—but was there no longer.

Bewildered, Baudelaire heard, from somewhere behind him,
the creak of a saddle, the slight rattle of a horse's bit. Crouched,
he looked around over his shoulder—and he rose slowly, turning, incredulous.

Sun rays, piercing aslant now between the trunks of the tall
trees, lit all the damp woodland with a radiant glow.

The man astride Baudelaire's hired horse, now untethered
from the tree bough, wore a caped gray greatcoat and a tall
black beaver hat.

He turned to Baudelaire the face of one marked for misfortune—the haggard mask of tragedy.

For a long moment, in the dew-gemmed glory of the morning
woods, they gazed at each—across a gulf no words or hands could
bridge.

All was lost.

Poe turned the horse's head, and the horse moved away at a
walk, and they passed from Baudelaire's view into the jigsaw
deeps of the leafing trees.

He could not believe it. He stood there motionless, in his
purple-lined cape, his silk hat, with his gold-knobbed stick in a
pink-gloved hand.

His American?

From the group about the carriages, on the greensward behind him, voices reached him—seeming remote, like voices in a dream—through the screen of laurels.

"Monsieur Sue—*who*, then, is this man I have killed?"

"General Aupick, I do not know the dead man's name."

"Kate, that hand dangling from the carriage window—d'you recognize that ring?"

"Why, yes, it's—*our* ring, Henry!"

Baudelaire turned slowly, numb. He looked through the laurel tangle, saw the man called Duprez withdrawing his head and shoulders from the door, now open, of Eugène Sue's carriage.

"Strange," said the man called Duprez. "He has our ring, Kate—and he has my watch and fob. But no—this is *not* the man I met at The Shamrock House on the New York waterfront."

General Aupick said, "Let *me* take a closer look at him." He thrust his head into the dim interior of the carriage. His voice sounded hollow from it: "He has an identical blemish on his cheek—but no, this is *not* the man who faced my pistol! And—this fellow's *stone cold!*" He drew back sharply from the carriage, turned to Sue. "There's no wound whatever in that man's chest! So I ask you, Monsieur Sue, why was *this* wadded in his shirtfront?"

He held up, in the sunshine, the blood-stained napkin.

"I cannot answer," said Eugène Sue.

"You cannot answer?" General Aupick said. "Monsieur Sue, I *demand* your explanation!"

"I sincerely regret, General," Sue said, "I am not at liberty to give it."

Baudelaire looked back over his shoulder into the deep woods, shining and still.

He was alone now.

He drew in his breath. Abruptly, he thrust his way through the laurels, stepped out into the open.

"All right, General," he said. "*I* will explain—if that is the right word."

"Charles!" said Caroline.

"I should prefer, General," Baudelaire said, not looking at her, "to do it—man to man."

"Then come!" General Aupick said, iron-hard.

He threw down the blood-stained napkin, strode out toward the center of the greensward.

"Charles," Caroline said again, distressed. "Charles—"

She moved toward him, holding out her hands for his.

But Baudelaire said, "No—stay there, Mother. This is my affair now." He half-smiled, with the bitterness of that self-knowledge which marks the end of youth. "It was *always* my affair."

He walked out to face General Aupick, awaiting him between the squares of the two handkerchiefs lying near the open pistol box on the damp grass.

In the sun-bright stillness, a thrush sang.

But under a gray sky far to the north of Paris, late the following afternoon, a parliament of rooks circled on slow, dark wings, harshly chorusing "Caw! Caw!" to a thin rain falling.

Bleak plowland, swept over by a mist of rain veils, sloped away up to a ridge fringed by thin, tall, pollarded poplars silhouetted against the sky. Over the tufted treetops the homing rooks circled and chorused, while others of their kind, all harshly cawing, still trod and pecked, flapped up from and alighted upon the wet plowland.

Rearing up solitary from the hedgerowed edge of the great field stood a gaunt signpost.

Hoofbeats sounded, growing louder. Their steady trot mingled with the harsh chorus of the rooks, and through the rain a horse bearing a rider in a caped greatcoat and a tall beaver hat drew level with the plowland—and continued as far as the finger post, where the rider reined in.

Coughing into the handkerchief pressed to his moustache, he looked up with hollow eyes at the words on the finger post:

ROUEN

LE HAVRE

The horse tossed its head, blowing through flared nostrils, and the rider, pocketing his handkerchief, stroked the taut tendons of the horse's neck. Through his damp black glove, with its hole in the forefinger, the rider felt the horse's soaking wetness —and was troubled by it, knowing that he had nothing else he might barter, for a steerage passage across the Atlantic, but this horse not his.

Not his! The story of his days: Had anything, in all the uncaring world, ever been his—except the burden of guilt, growing always heavier, which rode upon his back?

Why? *Why?* What mark of ordained misfortune was imprinted on him?

He looked up at the slow-moving cloud drifts coming in from the ocean. Already he could taste salt on his lips.

Escape was an illusion. Freedom was an empty dream.

He watched the rooks circling over the treetops on the ridge, and looked at the birds that still trod and pecked and cawed on the plowland furrows.

Two women, a young one and an old one—abandoned in Philadelphia: What had become of them?

Among the rooks on the furrows was another bird, seemingly shunned by its fellows, though of a kind with them, but greater than its kindred, longer-legged than they, and more cruelly beaked.

"*Corvus Corax,*" the rider said. "I know you. I know you, brother!"

• *200* •

His hollow gaze rested briefly on the bird, then he slapped his bridle sharply on his horse's neck.

The horse broke again into a trot, going northward where the fingerpost pointed.

Horse and rider faded into the rain veils, and the beat of the departing hoofs was lost in the continuous cawing of the rooks and the harsh, ironic croak of the raven.

Twenty-one

"Do you know," said Baudelaire, "why I've translated the tales of Poe with such care, such diligence, such patience?"

"How else could we have lived?" said Jeanne.

Wearing slippers and a blowsy wrapper, she lay among the cushions of her ottoman, idly picking hairs from the papier-mâché scalp of the gorilla, for she had been thinking vaguely about her solitary triumph as a prima ballerina.

Since *Sheba and the Beast,* engagements had grown less and less frequent for her. It was years now since she had danced, and she had put on a good deal of comfortable flesh. But Baudelaire, who was sitting at his writing table, had grown gaunt.

"Your answer, Jeanne," he said, "is typical of you. You have execrable taste."

"What I said, Charles, is true."

"Up to a point," said Baudelaire. "Yes, I was the first Frenchman to discover Poe's macabre tales, recognize their merit, and translate them into French. But it wasn't just to earn money, Jeanne. It was because I could see in his work—something of my own nature. He was *like* me, Jeanne."

He was not thinking of his physical appearance, though in fact, paler now, cleanshaven these days, his suit a threadbare black, he had come to look more like Poe than he knew.

His bachelor apartment in the Hôtel Lauzun, like Jeanne's exotic little love nest in the Place Dauphine, was long gone. They had lodgings now in a house on the Quai Voltaire. Much water had flowed under the gray stone bridges of the Seine, and few relics of a dandy's past survived in the room where they sat: his writing table, Jeanne's coffee table with the bamboo pipes and the censer bowl on it, Baudelaire's books cramming the shelves, and on the floor two prayer rugs showing worn patches. There was little else in the room, and the curtains of red velvet that framed the tall window and the fading daylight were shabby now.

"It's a shame," Jeanne said idly, "you never met him, Charles."

"Did I not?" said Baudelaire. "I wonder."

He picked up the letter that informed him of Poe's death.

"His mother-in-law," Baudelaire said. "Mrs. Maria Clemm. She has the handwriting of a very elderly woman. And she's sent me these things—works of his, printed pages torn from obscure periodicals. 'A few things of Eddie's,' she says, that I 'might like to have.'"

"She hopes you'll translate them," said Jeanne. "She says she's all alone now in—where is it?"

"A place called Fordham, in the state of New York," said Baudelaire. "Yes, she probably needs money. And where am I to get money, Jeanne?"

"Monsieur Ancelle," said Jeanne, and plucked a hair from the gorilla's scalp as viciously as if it had been the jurist's.

"Ancelle?" said Baudelaire wryly. "Mayor of Neuilly, these days—with talk of a street there to be named for him. A street! Such are the rewards of blameless mediocrity!" He smiled sardonically. "How often can I squeeze a centime out of Monsieur Ancelle? Every Quarter Day my creditors are clustered on his doorstep to collect their compound interest on my ancient debts. Compound interest—the garotte that strangles slowly. Ah, Jeanne, he was so right about that—my American!"

"There's your mother," Jeanne suggested.

"She sends what she can," said Baudelaire, "when she can do it without the general knowing. My mother, bless her! Ambassador's lady! How that must please her gay and frivolous heart!"

"She called me," said Jeanne, "your equatorial concubine. Oh, *la, la!*" She giggled.

"The general was lucky to survive the revolution of 'Forty-eight," Baudelaire said grimly.

Hatred of Aupick still rankled in him. He could not remember without shame how, in the 1848, when he was under the influence of drugs, he had brandished a musket and sought to inflame a street mob with shouts of *"Aux Invalides!* Asassinate General Aupick!"

The general had heard of that, undoubtedly, though he never had communicated again with his stepson since the duel in the Bois de Boulogne.

Jeanne said, "Eugène Sue might—"

"Eugène?" said Baudelaire. "A respectable member, since the 'Forty-eight revolution, of the Chamber of Deputies! I decline to go to Eugène hat in hand for money! My God, Jeanne, the contrasts in life! The general—Ambassador. Monsieur Ancelle —Mayor. Eugène Sue—a respected parliamentarian. And I— what have I to show? A prosecution for obscenity, on the grounds of my collected poems, my *Fleurs du Mal,* and the book's suppression! I—who swore posterity would have to reckon with me! There's irony, Jeanne."

Out of the growing dimness in the room as the daylight failed, Jeanne said, "Will you translate those things the old American lady sent?"

"I don't know," said Baudelaire. "They trouble me. This essay, 'Diddling Considered as One of the Exact Sciences'— Jeanne, those words sound echoes in my mind. I heard *my* American speak those very words. And here—this story the old lady's sent—'The Great Balloon Hoax'—about men crossing the Atlantic, from Europe to New York, in three days, by balloon. Did this story germinate from—'a touch of judicious harlequinade'— in the Luxembourg Gardens?"

"Charles, you think too much!"

"My American," said Baudelaire. "If his plot had succeeded, everything might have been so different! Jeanne, was *my* American Poe himself?"

"If he was," said Jeanne, "why did he not say so when he answered the letter you sent, care of the *New York Daily Mirror*, asking for permission to translate his tales?"

"He was proud, Jeanne. At bottom, Henri was as proud as Lucifer—and there was the matter of the horse."

"The horse?"

"He took the horse," said Baudelaire, "and left me the debt for it. And he was proud—a proud, strange, unhappy man. My translations of Poe's works have given you and me our bread and butter, Jeanne, these past few years. Yet if my American and Poe were one and the same man, I may never know it now, never be sure—because, by God, of a livery-stable horse!"

"You could ask the old lady," Jeanne said, "if she has any kind of portrait or likeness of her late son-in-law."

"Yes, I'll write to her, if and when I can send her a little money." Baudelaire smiled grimly. "I, too, still have a rag of pride."

He opened a thick notebook on the cover of which was the scrawled title *Journaux Intimes*. He turned the pages of manuscript, dipped in the inkwell a gold-nibbed, pink-dyed quill, his final remaining affectation; and under the latest entry in the book, he scribbled, "Write to Maria Clemm."

He laid down the quill on the open book, rose slowly and went to the window. Evening was closing in, windless and still. The clip-clop of hoofs sounded from below on the Quai Voltaire. Not yet were the lamps of passing carriages lighted, or the gas globes on the standards that lined the banks of the Seine. Across the river, slow-flowing under its gray stone bridges, smoke from the Tuileries chimneys rose thinly, untroubled, into the fading pallor of the sky.

"Words," Baudelaire said, "that I thought *I* had written —Poe had written before me. Dreams I thought were mine alone he had dreamed before ever I knew them. Poe *changed* me, Jeanne."

"Draw the curtains, Charles," Jeanne said. "Shut out the world."

"And the thousand ills of Fortunatus," Baudelaire said. *"His* words."

He drew the worn velvet curtains, and turned. In the room, now dark, glowed a small rose of fire, for Jeanne had fanned the charcoal in the censer bowl on the coffee table. Sitting on her ottoman, the grace of her lost youth sheathed now in flesh, she was leaning forward, preparing a pipe, the glow from the charcoal faintly illumining her beestung lips and the ebony sheen of her plump face.

"The hour of the poppy," Baudelaire said, "to open the gates of our artificial paradise."

He went to the ottoman, struck the gorilla head to the floor, where it fell with a thud, rolled, and lay leering with jungle fangs from the shadows.

Baudelaire sat down beside Jeanne, and with his chin cupped in his hands, the lock of hair, still dark, slanting across his brow, gazed somberly into the glow of the censer bowl.

"Edgar Poe," he said, "show me your face. I summon you —Edgar Poe!"

"Stop thinking," said Jeanne.

But the memory of one of the tales he had translated returned to Baudelaire. He murmured, " 'Masque of the Red Death,' " and a scene came to life for him in the small inferno— a rout of revelers in medieval motley and a frenzied dance, strident in their merriment, for they sought forgetfulness of plague at large in their contaminated world.

Among them, Baudelaire recognized himself as he once had been—young, handsome, gorgeously attired, his hands in pink-silk gloves clasping Jeanne, slender again, sleekly sinuous, alluring as a bacchante with slanted, amber eyes.

Now, one by one, the wild dancers froze to stillness, becoming aware of a figure in their midst—a sudden stranger garbed in crimson, at his hip a belted dagger with a jeweled hilt. They fell back from him as he moved slowly among them, searching, searching—until he paused, turning his pale, impassive, beautiful face on the young Baudelaire.

"I was mortal, but am fiend," the stranger said, with lips unmoving, fixed in a slight cold smile. "I was merciless, but am pitiful."

"This hideousness is insufferable," the young Baudelaire answered. "How can I sleep again?"

"Thou canst not rest for the cry of these great agonies?" the stranger said. "Then come with me into the Outer Night, and let me unfold to thee the graves."

"Show me thy face!" said the young Baudelaire.

The stranger raised a pale hand—and removed his beautiful, smiling mask from—

"Charles!" Jeanne said sharply. "You look so strange— what do you see in the fire there?"

"A skull," said Baudelaire.

The scene was gone. There was only the charcoal glowing red in the censer bowl, with slight crackling sounds.

"Stop wondering," said Jeanne.

Baudelaire smiled grimly, the fire shine reflected in his dark eyes as he watched the pellet in the tweezers Jeanne held begin to bubble blackly over the glow of the charcoal.

"No, Jeanne," he said. "I shall wonder—all my days."

Postscript

If in fact a meeting ever occurred between Poe and Baudelaire (first European to recognize the merit of Poe's tales of the macabre and first to translate them into a foreign language, French), no biographer of either man appears to have reliable evidence of it.

So, if such a meeting took place, it would seem only to have been possible during those four ambiguous months of 1844, in Poe's otherwise well-documented life —and at a time, moreover, when he was up to his old game of using a name not his own.

Certainly, Baudelaire repeatedly expressed a feeling —such was the influence of Poe's work upon him—that somewhere at some time, he had known the man personally.

Of those four doubtful months in 1844, never explained satisfactorily, Poe later claimed that he never had left New York. But when he was in his cups, he was apt to tell a strange story about having been to Europe, where, in Paris, he had fought a duel in which, in some way unspecified, Eugène Sue was involved.

In vino veritas?

It appears to be an open question. Hence the foregoing fantasy.

Poe's recurring military fixation; his urge to involve

himself in the Russo-Polish conflict; the sequestration in the hands of Monsieur Ancelle of Baudelaire's patrimony; Baudelaire's hatred of General Aupick for this reason (strengthened by suspected Oedipal complications); and all statements made regarding Aupick, Caroline, Ancelle, and Eugène Sue's career before and after the 1848 revolution, are factual; and Poe is known to have retained his West Point greatcoat until the end of his life.

The profound change in Baudelaire, the change that turned him from a mother's pampered boy and fashionable young dandy into the gaunt, embittered man of the famous portrait in the Paris gallery of the Orangerie, seems to have begun, almost abruptly, in 1844.

"The Gold Bug" was first published in 1843, "The Raven" in the latter half of 1844, when Poe, resurfacing from wherever he had been, became subeditor of the New York Daily Mirror, edited by Nathaniel P. Willis.

No railroad existed in Spain in 1844, but experimental lines were in operation in France.

Baudelaire's translations of Poe's macabre tales began to appear in Paris in 1847.